JOURNEY THROUGH INTERSTELLAR SPACE

VOLUME 1: MISSION TO MARS

AKSHITA CHANGKAKOTI

Made with ♥ on the Notion Press Platform
www.notionpress.com

Dedicated to the dreamers, stargazers, and fearless explorers who find inspiration in the boundless wonders of the cosmos. May this book ignite your imagination and take you on an extraordinary journey through the vast expanse of space. Here's to the adventurers who believe that the universe is an open book waiting to be explored, one celestial page at a time!

The Author

Contents

Contents

Acknowledgements

I express my heartfelt gratitude to my parents for their unwavering support throughout my authorial journey. Their encouragement has been my primary source of motivation, urging me to explore every horizon and avoid limiting myself to a singular pursuit. A sincere thank you to my teachers, whose imparted knowledge and tools have played a pivotal role in shaping my ability to write these books. As I present my third book, I hope readers will shower it with their love and appreciation!

Akshita Changkakoti

Appreciation from the INDIA BOOK OF RECORDS

Prologue

Technology has improved a lot over the past few years. Now, the influential organisation SCI-CORP, the leader in technology, has taken on a mission to colonise the Moon. New mining gear and power generators are being loaded onto the spacecraft. SCI-CORP has officially announced the launch of the mission in three days.

SCI-CORP is quite ambitious considering they had just been through a scandal in which their Archeological and Historical sector were discarded and given away to the Cult of Harrison who's public image has been improving since the scandal.

The Cult is currently running an investigation of a mysterious ruin the location of which is unknown. They have claimed to discover 'brilliant things' at the sight but refuse to disclose this information to the public. The ruin in question was shrouded in rumors just a few months ago. These rumors, based on facts or not, stated the sight to be of extraterrestrials.

SCI-CORP is sending researchers from Team SSTR who are Sue Susan, Samuel Johnson, Lily Carter and Lucy Abott. This particular team has risen the ranks quickly after entering the organisation and has shown incredible results.

Let's sit back and watch what unfolds.

I

The Disaster!

SCI.CORP, the largest research organization to date in 2034. By now, there have been quite some advances in the scientific field – the above organization's contributions were most significant.

SCI.CORP has really only faced one real threat in its surprisingly short history which nearly led to their decline. After level-headed actions however, the threat soon subsided and fell under the wraps up until now...

This is where Sam, Lucy, Sue and Lily come in. They were researchers working in the Steller Research Field. There were different teams in all fields – due to the work being segregated, the organization could accomplish a whole lot more than its competition. They were in Team SSTR.

Teams with the prefix of SS (short for Specialised Service-oriented) are ranked above almost all of the staff. They were given more important tasks. At the moment, there were only 10 teams with the prefix of SS based on performance. This prefix was also given to the teams that were problematic. The difference was that these teams' titles ended with an S or T. There are only 3 of such teams.

In total there are 13 teams with this prefix.

RS (Research-oriented Specialised) teams ranked just below SS. Followed by RS were IW (Introductory Work) teams which were the base level teams people got assigned to after joining.

Now, we come to the present day while the team is getting ready to board the ship to their rocket to the Moon for their new mission – Moonscape. When it happened...

There was a bang! Then a large burst of greenest yellow smoke came rushing through. And in a moment's notice, it seemed as though the world had gone black.

The next moment, there was a putrid smell in the air. And outside the window, was what looked like a nuclear wasteland; some structures were intact as much as possible.

And in minutes, SCI.CORP's staff began to panic. The friends (Team SSTR) were just standing there looking at what remained – almost desolate landscape.

"Quit staring! We better tell Dr John and Smith," said Lily trying to divert their attention.

"You are 'practical' for once!" said Sue.

"I always am! You know very well that I am right!"

"No need to be such hotheads, let's go, tell them now," said Sam, taking the lead. "How could this...?" said Lucy who was scared and shocked (reasonably) at what had happened, followed Sue and Lily who were walking behind Sam.

They reached the office which was a few floors up after a few minutes.

"May we come in?" asked Sam, entering half way.

"Yes, yes, come in," said Dr John, relatively unfazed even though two walls in his office were of windows.

Separated by a wall which did not join the window on the other side was Dr Smith's office. Dr Smith was again reasonably more astonished.

"There seems to be a problem – as you can see," said Lily signaling to the window Dr John and Smith were facing.

"Well... It was inevitable," said Dr John, finally looking up from his desk on which there were numerous sheets of paper.

"Inevitable?! Is that all you have got to say?" said Dr Smith.

"Well, you know that... And anyways they were partnered up with the wrong 'investors'. Just won't listen! I tried to warn them; I tried but by then they were already too thick in the skull to even care!" said Dr Jones.

"I do know that... but isn't this too sudden?" said Dr Smith "It has just been 5 years."

"Well, it has also been 5 years since the other organization partnered up with them,"

"What are you talking about?" asked Lucy, finally interrupting Dr John and Smith.

"That is not our concern now. We better prepare to leave this planet," began Dr John "As you know, this sort of environment is not ideal for living."

"I agree with you on that but where will we go? There are few possible options at the moment," said Lily.

"Well said! Let us think. Sue and Lily, you check the options. Sam, Lucy go and stop the commotion downstairs," instructed Dr Jones.

"Yes!"

Sam and Lucy headed out to give an announcement for the staff to keep calm. Soon, everyone was at work for an evacuation. They all were now waiting for further instructions to move into the rockets.

Meanwhile, Lily and Sue had found an answer.

"We could go to Mars. It has frozen water, a similar environment and it has more resources," said Lily looking up from her tablet.

"Agree," said Sue who wanted to beat Lily to it by saying the same.

"Well, good job. We will get ready to evacuate," said Dr Smith "You both get Sam and Lucy and turn on the solar-powered rockets."

"Wait, those?" asked Sue.

"Yes, those," repeated Dr Smith.

Lily and Sue got Sam and Lucy and turned on the rockets.

"Load all electronics, supplies and flora and fauna now!" came an announcement.

Everyone hurried to load all the capsules – SCI.CORP used capsules at least as big as entire flats to store animals and plants – on to the ships.

They got everything loaded in about 3 to 4 hours. Now, the base – the place where they are working – the protective field was weakening. The base of the organization had a protective field which is a dome that surrounds the facility – a large multi-building complex with living quarters and all.

II

Lift Off! The Journey through Space!

After a few short hours, the spacecraft were in space. Then onwards, everyone on board promptly got to work. Tasks were assigned and everything looked as though they had never left Earth.

"Well then, we better get to work as well," said Sam getting off his seat and picking up his things. "We have two tasks for now," began Sue "They are due by the end of today."

"What are they?" asked Lily as picked up her things. "Sorting files and some code," said Sue as she headed out.

"That should be simple right? I mean me and Sue are the best at sorting," said Lucy. "Then you two should be able to handle that. I will do the code," said Lily "And yes, Sam, you are working too!"

"Ugh, fine!" said Sam as they all headed for their quarters to get to work.

"Sam! Come to the lab, I need you to help me design a suit," said Dr. Smith, calling out behind them.

"Wha, What?! Can repeat?" said Sam as he slowed down to a halt.

"Well, head over to the lab with me," said Dr Smith leading the way.

"Sure!" said Sam "I guess I am not coding today!"

"Sure, sure, I would get faster anyway. Bye!" said Lily, rushing off.

"Okay, bye!" said Sam, heading off "Why do we need new suits again?"

"The old ones were damaged by the radiation and the ones that were intact went missing," explained Dr Smith.

"Missing?" asked Sam. "Long story. We better get to work," said Dr Smith.

"Sure! I already have an idea on the draft," said Sam as he entered the lab and got to work.

After a few hours, the prototype was ready and Sam headed back to meet up at the cafeteria.

III

A Surprise!

They all took their meals and sat down at a table in the staff common room. Sam was the first to start eating. "Wow! These are much, much better than the canned ones! I am just now realizing how good baked beans are!" he clamored as scooped up another spoonful.

"You're right! The canned ones are horrible! They taste like rotten baked beans!" declared Lucy as she continued to eat.

"Well, I was not quite for your vegan craze, but I definitely agree with this. And I am just curious, did you eat rotten baked beans before?" said Sue as she took another bite.

"Ummm... yeah that was when I was in college. I was also in poverty apparently because my allowance was basically worth one dollar. So, when I bought something, it never went to waste," replied Lucy.

"No wonder, you were a thrifty person since college and I studied with you, so I know you had a fair allowance," disproved Lily as she stuffed her face with food.

"Lucy, no wonder you were vegan. You wanted to save some cash" teased Sam.

"Come on! Sam used disposable dishes until he graduated! And I am thrifty right?" argued Lucy.

"Well, I didn't eat spoiled food unlike you," argued Sam.

"Yeah" added Lily "Eating spoiled food is a bit overboard don't you think?"

Just then Dr. Jones rushed into the room. "An urgent alert! We will be landing tomorrow. The statistics had malfunctioned!" he said as he reached their table.

"What!? So, you're saying we guessed the wrong time! What do we do now?" asked Lily, surprised as she made room for him to sit.

"There was a bug in the system and we had just solved it. Sam, would you mind distributing suits?" Dr Jones explained just before he jumped from his seat and hurried to make an announcement to the rest of the crew.

"Sam, what suits is he talking about, we already have our space suits. And was this the 'work' you had?" asked Lily as she finished off the baked beans.

"Um... yeah, I had to design a new type of suit as the others could not handle radiation as discovered after the explosion. I had to design one for the Mars environment. It had to be radiation-proof, at least more resistant to be sustainable on Mars and-" Sam began.

"Sam, umm, can you cut it short? I believe we are running out of time" said Sue as she got up. "Yeah, we better get ready and secure the dorms, come on Lucy let's go! We don't want our stuff to get wrecked" said Sue as she raced off to the dormitories.

"Hey! Wait up!" called out Lucy as she raced behind her.

"Well, I better get to distributing. This is a bummer since we were planning to watch something tonight," Sam complained as he headed off to the lab.

"For once, I will help you. I know it's gonna take forever for you to do it – as expected- and if we want to have fun tonight, we better hurry," said Lily as she followed.

At the lab, they went through the boxes.

"Wow! These suits are much better than the ones we had before. Can't wait to let Sue and Lucy take a look!" remarked Lily as they headed out.

"Yeah... I wanted to change the design anyways and so-," Sam began as he distributed suits from the box he was holding.

"No need to explain, cut the lecture short sometimes, Sam," said Lily as she distributed the suits in the box she was holding.

"Great! My new design seems to be better than the last suit designer's design. Yes!" said Sam as he went to get another box.

"Well, good job on that one. I guess," said Lily as she went to get another box "Oh! All the boxes are empty which means we are done!"

"Sam, did you get suits for us and Sue and Lucy?" asked Lily as she wiped her forehead.

"Oh yeah! Forgot. Don't worry I'll get some from the production area now," said Sam as he dashed off. After a minute or so he was back with the suits.

"Oh yeah and I got some intel," said Sam.

"Tell us in the dorm;now let's get going!" said Lily.

"Do you have your backpack?" asked Sam.

"Yeah, where's yours?" asked Lily.

"It's in my dorm. Dr Smith sent it there when we headed to the lab," replied Sam.

"Can you carry the suits?" asked Sam.

"Fine..." replied Lily as she stuffed the suits into her backpack.

They arrive at the dorm, a few minutes later. "We got the new suits and some intel," said Lily walking in.

"Yeah, it might or might not be related to the explosion," said Sam sitting down.

"What is it?" asked Lucy eagerly. "Well, when I asked Dr. Smith what happened to the suits we had before, he said that some of the suits were damaged and... some had gone missing!" said Sam.

"Missing? How?" asked Sue "Did you get any details?"

"If the suits had gone missing, someone had to have taken them," theorized Lily.

"That's right! And I have a feeling it is related to 'that woman'" beamed Lucy "Think about it! She might be aboard the ship so she had to be a researcher or someone important."

"You are right! She might have stolen them because of some ulterior motive. But she could not have been a researcher because why would she be out on that day. We were the only team who had a mission that involved getting outside. All other teams would have been ground staff. We were on the first Moon Colonization mission after all," said Sue.

"Then she might be someone important! We'll figure that out later." said Sam. "Now, we better get some sleep! Good night!" said Lily, slamming the door of her room and going to bed.

The others did the same and fell fast asleep.

IV

A Hasty Landing

The next day, at 7:00 AM, Dr. Smith made an announcement.

"All researchers and workers. I repeat. All researchers and workers, report to the secure landing seats by 11 o'clock sharp. All researchers and workers report by 11 o'clock sharp! The ship will land at approximately 12 o'clock. Keep all your belongings in your dorms. Only carry your tablet, laptop and phone. Kindly note! Any worker or researcher found absent or not at their positions will receive punishment! Kindly note! Any absent employee or anyone out of their positions will receive punishments such as paycheck cuts."

This woke the friends up.

"WHAT?! WE ARE LANDING TODAY?!" exclaimed Sam as hurried to get ready.

"Oh my gosh! I am so, so excited! New assignments... projects and... and tasks!! Yay!" exclaimed Lucy as she got out of bed.

"Well, I did distribute the suits yesterday so it only makes sense that we land today," remarked Lily as she had some coffee.

"Come on! Let us get some breakfast quickly! We must get to the landing seats by 11," reminded Sue as she got out of the dorm. The others followed her with their stuff.

After they had breakfast, they went to the landing seats. Just as they took their seats, it was 11 O'clock.

"Thank God! We made it on time! No paycheck cuts today!" said Sam as he got comfortable in his seat.

"Yeah! I didn't want a fine. I am saving up for a new game," said Lily who was already on her phone.

"Me too! I really need to get more equipment" Sue said as she sat down.

"I REALLY CAN'T WAIT TO GET TO MARS! All the WORK IN THE WORLD!!" exclaimed Lucy as she took out her camera and notebook.

"Lucy, don't you think shouting is going a bit overboard on the excitement?" said Lily.

"Chill out, there are other people on the ship," said Sam.

After an hour's wait, the landing procedure began.

"Sam, are the landing pads in place?" asked Dr. Jones as he began to land the ship.

"Yes sir!" replied Sam.

The ships soon landed.

"Wow, Mars is so much better than I thought it would be," said Lily as she put her phone down.

"This is it! We are finally here!" exclaimed Sue.

"I LOVE THIS PLACE! I have already made a virtual fact file!" yelled Lucy as she began taking notes like crazy while uploading the files to her tablet.

"Well, better stay where you all are. We will be reorganizing the ships into positions. I repeat, kindly remain at your seats!" ordered Dr. Smith.

After a little turbulence, they finally landed.

"All right, all the groups will be assigned tasks daily. They will be mostly building tasks; so don't worry," said Dr. Smith as he started to assign tasks.

"What will we do today? I don't think we can do this all today," asked Sam as he glanced at the now full tasks log.

"Yeah, the tasks log is quite full. Are you sure we will be doing it all today?" added Lily. "Yeah, is that all for us?" said Lucy, hoping for extra work.

"Don't worry, I have labeled the tasks date wise; so, you will be doing one daily," clarified Dr. Jones.

"Yes, you might get extra assignments because there is much work to do. Kindly cooperate," added Dr. Smith.

"Sure, and I guess we have two tasks today. They seem pretty interesting!" said Lucy as checked the tasks log.

"Wait! ONLY TWO! Great!" said Sam as he put his tablet back on its stand.

"Um, Sam, we have to construct and design a new farming and building bot for the Mars colonization plan" reminded Lily as she stared at the log.

"Uuh umm oh no!" pouted Sam as he got up.

"Well great! I had dreamed of this!" exclaimed Sue as she jumped out of her seat.

"Me too!! We have, like the best assignment ever!" exclaimed Lucy as she jumped from her seat.

"Sue, Lucy, I think you are the only ones excited about this," said Sam as he too got up.

"Come on guys! Don't you guys' even care?!" relented Sue.

"Chill... We will get to work now, ok!" assured Lily.

V

A Lot to Do

"Well, the first step, as always, is getting materials. Let's go to the hardware department," instructed Sam as he took the lead.

"What will we need?" asked Sue curiously as she and the others followed Sam.

"I mostly work at the Hardware Department; I will deal with that. Send me the blueprints for building later." replied Sam "You guys can start on the blueprints and software at the lab. I will be back in a bit. Bye!" Sam went off to the Hardware Department.

"So, who's programming? And who's designing?" asked Sue as they headed towards the lab.

"Well, I am better at designing; so, I will go with making the blueprints. And you guys can do the software. You ok with that?" answered Lucy as she glanced at some previous designs.

"'Sure! Of course, I am not" replied Lily.

"Come on! I am really not that bad!" argued Sue.

"Yeah right!" slouched Lily.

"Come on! Let's get to work already," said Lucy as she led the way to the lab.

"Let us get our laptops and get to work! Don't sweat it, Lily!" assured Sue as she took the lead and ran ahead.

"Hey! Slow down!" said Lucy as she ran behind her.

"Wait up, Sue!" called out Lily as she followed.

"Finally! Let's get started!" exclaimed Sue once they entered the lab.

"It's now or never," said Lily as she got to work.

"Our work is so, so interesting!" reminded Lucy as she got to work on the blueprint paper.

"No need to brag. I will get the software done earlier than you, just you see!" challenged Lily as she immediately began working.

"I don't think this is really that easy, Lily," remarked Sue as she got to work.

"Well, it's hard for you," argued Lily.

"Come on! Stop grumbling and get to work!" instructed Lucy.

"Well, Lucy, I hate to break it to you but you're the one not working," reminded Sue.

"Now I understand, Lily," said Lucy as got back to work.

They worked for a long time. And finally completed one bot design and programming.

"I will work on the programming too then we will be able to work faster," said Sue.

They reached the warehouse and took the rovers to the lab. At the lab, they met Sam who brought in the materials.

"Lucy, are the blueprints ready? I brought the materials" said Sam as he came in.

"Yeah, here they are," said Lucy, handing over the blueprints. I will help you out," said Lucy.

"We can help you guys when we are done early," suggested Sam as he began building the bot.

After a few hours, everyone had finished their tasks. "Whew! That took forever. I hope this is all we have to do," Lily said as she drank some water.

"Yeah, me too! And it's already 7:25," remarked Lucy as she finished her water.

"Yeah, we should go submit the tasks and have dinner, right?" suggested Sam as he stacked the bots onto the service trays.

After stacking up all the bots on trays, they started stacking the trays onto trolleys.

"Whew! That took long enough!" said Sue as she wiped her forehead.

"Now let's go, drop them off!" said Lucy as she started pushing one of the trolleys.

The others followed suit. "We better eat fast if we want to watch something later. Better not argue about what to eat, Lucy" said Sam as he checked the menu.

After a few minutes, they submitted their tasks.

They headed to the canteen and had dinner. After that, they headed to their dorms.

"Don't disturb me. I will be staying up late. You guys can sleep if you want," said Lily as she plopped onto her bed and began gaming.

"Right, whatever. I am going to bed. Cannot be late for work," said Lucy as she closed her door and went to bed.

"Me too," said Sue as she shut her door and headed to bed.

"I am staying up," said Sam as he locked his door.

Lily shut her room's door and hopped on her bed.

VI

A Surprise Awaits!

"Guys! I have great news! We have a group project," said Lucy as she rushed into the dorm.

"What is it? ... It is too early even for me. What is it?" said Sue as she got out of bed.

"It's important, da!" said Lucy as she brought their suits in along with some other gear.

"Why did you bring all this stuff in, and what are we going to do with it?" asked Sam as he came back from the canteen with a cup of coffee.

"Yeah, what is it with you waking people up so early? And what is it we have to do again?" asked Lily "Sam, did you bring one for me?".

"Yeah, here," said Sam as he handed her a coffee.

"Now then, Lucy. What work did we have?" asked Sue as she got out of her room fully dressed in work clothes.

"We will be exploring and building on the surface of Mars in person! This is going to be so... so amazing!" Lucy began to explain with great excitement. "And did I mention we will test new equipment too? I just can't wait any longer! What are you all waiting for? I have already ordered breakfast for us all and-,"

"Lucy! It is 6 in the morning! Let us get ready first then we'll talk about that. And you just woke me up so... you're paying for my lunch today," declared Lily as she got out of bed.

"Come on! Do not be so mean I convinced Dr. Jones to assign us this mission instead of building more bots," Lucy argued back.

"Let's get breakfast and talk about this here," said Sue, and she headed out.

At the canteen, they discussed the work.

"So, what exactly do we have to do?" asked Lily.

"We have to explore Mars terrain and help get the rovers there and then have them get used to the terrain," explained Lucy "We also have to help in building some basic protection shields like the ones we had at the former facility."

"Oh, okay. We do have quite a lot of work in hand," remarked Sam as he finished eating.

"It is inevitable. We are on a mission, am I right?" said Sue merrily as she too finished eating.

"Well, you are right and this work does sound like fun!" admitted Lily.

"Well then, what are we waiting for? Let's get to work now!" said Lucy as she led the way to their dorm.

"Oh yeah. Sue, you didn't need to dress in that. We have to put on our special suits and clothes," added Lucy as they started changing into their suits.

"Is there a limit on the amount of land we can explore? Because the suits I made can extract oxygen from the outside environment," asked Sam as he got out of his room in the suit with the helmet in his arm.

"Yeah, about 10 kilometers away from the base for today," answered Lucy as she too headed out in her suit.

"Oh okay," added Sam.

"How do we talk?" asked Lily.

"We transmit our voice to the researchers around us," explained Sam.

"Don't we have to go now?" asked Sue as she entered the room.

"Yeah, but that can wait right, Lucy?" asked Lily as she too came out fully dressed.

"We will go in around 15 minutes." replied Lucy as she led the group to the exit. "We need to head to the exit area. Only researchers on missions like ours are allowed there since it's the most dangerous area on the ship".

"Oh. I never knew there was an exit" remarked Sam as he followed her.

"Me too. I can't believe we got so much work in one day," said Lily as she followed suit.

"Well, this is a great opportunity to prove our skill and if we are lucky, get a promotion," exclaimed Sue.

"You really do love this job a lot, huh." said Lily.

"Well, in order to buy your time at work, it is always easier if you like what you do," said Lucy.

"I guess you are right," admitted Lily.

"Wow! The area near the exit is cool," said Sam.

A long corridor lined with fire extinguishers, first aid kits and oxygen tanks led to the exit. The exit itself was an isolated room with a heavy locked door guarding it along with a guard or two. The door had many warnings plastered on it along with a poster displaying a set of rules.

The poster read:

Basic Safety Precautions

- No member of staff will be allowed entry if they are not here for a task, project etc.
- No member of staff will be allowed to enter without prior notice either for a rescue or servicing mission.
- Oxygen tanks are in the room beyond this door for emergencies.
- Any member of staff found using or tampering with these tanks will be put under house arrest.
- For any mission or task for coming here staff must first check if their suits are worn properly
- Any and all staff with improper suits will not be allowed to exit until they fix up their suits.

Poster with Rules

"Well, that's a lot of rules to just head outside," remarked Lily as she shrugged it off.

"The rules are there to protect us. I am glad the company put up so much effort to make our work easier," began Sue "Even if we are stranded here, we can still live a happy life if we want to. Isn't this para-,"

"Cut it short, Sue. We actually have to get to work, you know," reminded Sam.

"Stop. Let me check if your suits are on the right way," said the guard who was on shift at the time.

After their suits had been checked they headed for the exit. The exit was lined with bots.

"I don't know what is out there but this is a mission," said Lily.

"Relax, this is gonna be a whole lot of fun!" said Lucy as she stepped outside.

The others followed. The Martian terrain was bright orange. They took out and turned on the bots and began exploring.

"Where should the protective wall go?" asked Sam as he went to get it.

"About 10 kilometers away," replied Lucy as she went to get some materials.

"I will wait here for you guys," said Lily.

"Me too," said Sam.

Sue and Lucy went to get materials.

After a few hours, they were done building. When they tried to get through the door, it just wouldn't open. Lily even tried to open it with a crowbar.

"You guys locked the door, didn't you?" asked Sam.

"Um, yeah," admitted Sue.

"Does anyone have a phone... Wait, we can't use phones... Oh yeah, this is space. Sam, do your suits have any sort of communication?" asked Lily.

"Yes, luckily. Press the red button on your suit and it will send a message calling for help along with your location from the tracker on your suit," replied Sam. "You can also call a reporter with the blue button below it."

"Thank God! You remembered to put that in!" exclaimed Lily as she set off the alert.

Hours later, there was no response. "What on earth?!" exclaimed Sue.

"I am hungry!" moaned Lily "What is it with the service here?! If this goes on, we'll starve!"

Meanwhile, the reporter who was supposed to report on such incidents was fast asleep. Suddenly an alarm went off in the department beside the Report and Control department. This woke him up and then he saw their call.

Back on the surface of Mars, the friends were sitting on the ground, waiting for a signal.

Suddenly the door of the exit opened. They rushed in, ran past the guard, and took off their helmets.

"Whew! We are saved!" exclaimed Lucy. "By the way, what happened? I thought there was a reporter in charge of doing these things," asked Lily.

"Yeah, there is a reporter for that," recalled Sam.

"Well, we better check in with him ... or her because they are not doing a good job at all! People should be punctual about work and ta-," Sue began.

"Cut it short, where can we find that reporter?" asked Sam, interrupting Sue.

"I don't know. Maybe we should check the layout of the ship," suggested Lucy.

"Good idea!" said Lily as she checked a map of the ship which was pasted on the wall beside her.

"As you can see, I am a punctual worker who respects company poli-," Sue began the lecture.

"Hey! I am punctual and hard-working too!" interrupted Lucy.

"Cut it out! We all saw how punctual you two are when you locked the door and trapped us outside," said Sam.

"That was a one-off thing," explained Sue, stubbornly.

"Yeah!" added Lucy.

"That doesn't really matter," said Sam "We need to check in with the control group."

"I found it!" said Lily pointing to a place on the map.

"Well, we better get there now!" exclaimed Sue.

"Calm down," said Sam. The friends headed over to the control group's area and questioned who was responsible for keeping them locked out for a long time.

"They said that the reporter would be here somewhere," said Sam as he glanced at the walls looking for a symbol or something that would help them get there.

After a few minutes, they arrived. "Hey, is there any problem in the reporting center? Why did it take so long to open the door?" asked Sam as he entered.

"Sorry, that was my fault," said the reporter.

"Oh, I just wanted to check in," explained Sue.

The friends submitted photos from the outside terrain and completed the task.

Sue checked the tasks log. "We have another task guys. We have to check the soil composition," said Sue.

"What now?!" asked Lily. "Um, yeah," added Lucy. "Well, this is a bore," said Sam.

The friends put their helmets back on and took samples from the land inside the protective shield and went to the lab to test it.

While they were doing so, they saw a large group of people in spacesuits outside an exit from a large window in the lab. It was much larger than any team they had seen - Sue was pretty sure there were no teams with more than five people.

They were all standing around a strange device which was out of view.

"What the heck?" said Sam "What're they doing outside like that?"

"Don't know," said Sue, who wasn't looking anymore. "They are going to be dealt with anyway. Now focus, Sam!"

"Well, do we have any more tasks?" asked Lily as she finished work.

"Nah. Relax. We do have work tomorrow though," said Lucy.

"I need a break," complained Lily. The friends finished their work and went to their dorm to sleep.

VII

Construction Work

From the next day, work on the expansion of the base had begun. All workers were at work building structures for research and expansion. The friends are too busy at work readying a mining field with the help of the newly made construction bots.

"Well, this week has been tiring. Not only do we have 2 or 3 tasks, but we also have 1 or 2 extras daily," said Sam as took ice samples.

"Sam, did you find any radioactive materials in your area?" asked Lily who had been looking for a reliable fuel for the ship.

"Nah, but I did find water ice," said Sam. "Great! I was looking for that!" said Sue from an area to the right.

The friends completed their work after a few hours.

"Well, that was fun," said Lily, annoyed. "We will have work later so as to finish with the expansion quickly," said Sue.

"Team SSTR, report to the main office! I repeat. Team SSTR, report to the main office, now!" announced a reporter.

"What?! Now?!" exclaimed Lucy "Yes, yes, yes! We might get a new mission, new gear... new stuff, ne-,"

"We get it, Lucy. I am excited as well. We will get an opportunity to fine-tune our skills!" said Sue.

"You two really love your work, that's for sure but no need to brag about it," said Sam as he led the way.

"This better be good." Said Lily. The friends arrived at the main office. The main office had many researchers from different teams and branches present.

"Thank you for coming here on short notice. We wanted to discuss a problem with this team and some others," explained Dr Smith.

"Now that everyone is here, we can begin," said Dr Jones.

"We are short on resources such as iron and water. We need some special forces to head to the moon; temporarily to the Moon under the command of the newly appointed manager, Dr John. The forces will remain on the moon until a certain quota of supplies is collected. The forces will take a relatively small area of the farming and sanitation department. Groups will be assigned shortly. Kindly remain in the main office," explained Dr Jones.

The teams discussed the mission while the special teams were being formed. "Well, thank god this is a change of plans," said Lily. "Yeah! I was hoping to go to the moon too!" said Sue.

"You all will remain in the same groups with one senior officer. You will meet tomorrow so you may now head to your dorm rooms. You will be given further information tomorrow," concluded Dr Smith.

The friends headed back to their dorm room. "What do you think we will do next?" asked Lucy "I mean we might head out tomorrow or the day after," predicted Sam as he went to bed.

"Whatever! Good night!" wished Lily as she dozed off. "Good night!" wished Sam and Sue as they too dozed off. "Good night!" wished Lucy as she rolled around in bed trying to sleep. She was so, so excited that she stayed up all night.

VIII
Mission Moonscape

The next day, Lucy had gone to get breakfast. The others were getting ready to go. "Wonder why we have to go so early," said Sam as he got dressed. "That may be because of the mission," guessed Lily, who was already dressed. "We have to go to the common room to get further details," explained Sue who had checked the

"Of course, I am already good to go," bragged Sue. "I am back! I just got some sandwiches" exclaimed Lucy as she entered the room. "Thanks!" said Sue as she took a sandwich from Lucy.

The friends ate up and headed out to the common room. "We didn't need to bring anything... strange...," thought out loud Sam. "Well, that's a good thing," sighed Lily.

"Hello there!" waved a skinny middle-aged woman. "Um, hello, miss. Whom might you be?" asked Lucy as she headed over to her.

"You are team SSTR, am I correct?" asked the woman. "Yes, we are," said Sue. "Well then, greetings! I am your new invigilator and a member of your team," the woman said "I am Martina Goodwill."

"Wait, is this just for the mission or a permanent change?" asked Sam. "This is permanent. Let me explain. After an... incident where the teams failed to execute a task, all teams are required to have an invigilator," explained Martina as she took out a report on the 'incident' from her backpack to show them.

Case 346

Hazard Level – 10

Cause – Irresponsible workers.

   (Team SSRS)

Victims – NONE

Incident – Exit doors 1 & 2 were left open. Team SSRS failed to follow basic safety protocol. They were told to buffer the exit but due to the lack of monitoring the exit's air-tight door was broken.

Recovery Time – 1 DAY

Protocol Update – Invigilators are to be assigned to all teams to prevent more incidents*.

Incident Report

"Wait, what happened that day?!" exclaimed Lily "we had just gotten off work!"

"That's right! After you all headed out, Team SSRS entered the exit chamber and caused this wreck. Luckily, we were able to fix it after the meeting. After that drama, Team SSRS was disqualified and sent on Mission Moonscape. Dr

Jones said that they'd be less troublesome there," explained Martina.

"That's good to hear! Bad news for us since we might have to work with them. But what about the mission? We were supposed to meet here, right?" asked Sue. "Well, Dr Jones and Smith are running late I guess," Martina suggested.

"Are all the teams here?" asked Dr. Smith on the microphone "Good! We will be sending you all out on your mission today in the evening. You can go and collect your gear from the research lab. Get ready about 2 hours before boarding the miniature space crafts. Load up on materials and return to the ship as soon as possible. And your new invigilators will be living near your quarters. That's it for the instructions. You can head to your dorms!"

The teams slowly funneled out of the common room. "We should pick up our gear first," said Sue as she headed towards the storage room. The team got there and brought a few suits back to their dorm.

The moon suits, as they liked to call them, were heavier than the suits they wore on Mars because the Moon's gravitational force is weaker than that of the Earth. The suits also had oxygen tanks attached to the back because the Moon has a thin atmosphere.

The suits were also white like the typical space suit. The ones our friends had picked up were different from those they had on Earth; those were unusable by the time they got to Mars.

The friends headed back to the dorm. "By the way, how are we going to get rid of the still radioactive suits?" asked Sue.

"Maybe we could bury them deep in the soil," suggested Sam.

"We should tell Dr Jones or Dr Smith first," reminded Lucy.

"You're right. After the mission we should take care of that," said Lily as she went to get dressed knowing that the mission would begin soon.

"Hey! Team SSRS had been in another report. They had been the ones who had us build the protective wall after supposedly letting a junior on the Martian terrain without proper gear," said Sue.

"SSRS pops up a lot when you go through incident reports," said Lily, scrolling through reports on her tablet.

"You're right! They might have something to do with Martina. Isn't it suspicious that we suddenly get an invigilator? And that we only learn of this Team SSRS now? I haven't heard of it in any report for all the time I've been here," said Lily, glancing over at the screen.

"Yes, strange. You've been here the longest, you'd know. It seems that Team SSRS is new here. That too being suspicious as all the reports on them and their records come from after the explosion," said Sam, thoughtfully "It is quite suspicious."

"Boarding time! Get to your spacecraft immediately, following your invigilators, now!"

"We better get going! Sue said as she led the way.

The teams on the mission boarded the ships and settled down. The rockets used for this mission were much smaller than the ones that made up the base.

They were grey as well and could house just about enough people to make a base. Some of the researchers would live there and go back every month on shifts.

The friends and their invigilator had boarded the ship.

IX

Team SSRS

The friends had just got an invigilator, learnt about a suspicious team and were on their way to the Moon.

"Team SSRS seems to have been causing a lot of problems," said Sam, seeing if Martina knew of anything they did not.

"You're right, mate! They are trouble-makers! Naughty ones!" said Martina.

"Well, since they are coming with us, don't they have an invigilator?" asked Lucy.

"Well... They have something sorta like that...," whispered Martina, looking as though she shouldn't have said that.

"A leader? A head, what? Seems suspicious..." remarked Lily "Who might this 'invigilator' be?"

"Sorry, can't tell ya here. Meet me in our team dorm then no one'll know. It's a secret." whispered Martina "You see I've been looking into this too, y'know. I can also give ya some clues,"

"Great, then! We will meet up there!" said Sam.

"Now, shh! We can't be heard!" warned Sue.

A few minutes later, the ships took off. And began their journey. The friends moved into their dorm and locked the door so no one could hear.

Half grateful and half suspicious of Martina.

"Can you tell us what you know now?" asked Lily, locking the entrance.

"Yeah, yeah!" beamed Lucy.

"Well, Dr. Smith had told me to erase some files on a particular person. Their code was 1121, suspicious, no one has a code like that. No one's code had the suffix 12.

Don't know her name but thought that she'd done somethin' on that day, somethin' real bad! That's why she'd be erased from the database; that's jus' what I think.

I'd looked into some files and other stuff the other day and boy, was I surprised with what I found; this article! A small group of people wearing dark cloaks were spotted near the powerplant. It was one short second before they disappeared behind the powerplant.

And just before the explosion a mysterious group of figures had entered the facility.

This article you see was published by our opponents. They raise suspicion and create propaganda. Lucky, Dr John and Smith didn't let it get published. Those people were from a rival organisation. Sneaking in, like that. damaging our reputation!"

"Minimize suspicion, you say," began Lily "Firstly, whoever sneaked in would do it right before the explosion, likely! Oh yes and the people who sneaked in were damaging SCI.CORP's reputation? What do you mean by that?"

"They were framing the company! Naughty jerks! They wouldn't do this if they were good! The organisation has every right to keep this a secret!" repeated Martina.

"Could be pausable!" said Lucy.

"How exactly?" asked Sue.

"All this just confirms our suspicions! No accounts on framing are there in the records to this date," said Sam "Why would they have been let in if they were trying to ruin the organisation's reputation? And if they entered right before the 'explosion'. Wouldn't they know something? Or were they escaping?"

"Well... They... were.... They were... um, trusted, yeah trusted traders!" stammered Martina.

"Get your facts straight!" began Lily.

"Team SSTR, you have to report to the lab!" came an announcement interrupting their discussion.

"Oh! I completely forgot to tell ya! We gotta pick up our gear from the lab. Don't worry it's only one backpack's worth!" said Martina.

"Well, then me and LILY will go and pick them up!" said Sue, enthusiastically pulling Lily by the hand.

"Let me come too! I promise I'll help!" said Lucy as she followed the two to the door.

"Sure, why not! The more the merrier!" said Sue, locking the door behind her. The three of them headed to the lab.

By the time they got there, most of the gear sets had already been collected. The gear set included: mining equipment, a magnifying glass, laser cutters of different sizes, an emergency remote that to be used to call for help in case of an emergency, two first-aid kits and a guidebook.

Luckily enough of them were left. They quickly took their things and went back.

"We should not worry too much about 'that'. Getting to visit the Moon and all! I had hoped that we would get back on our Lunar Colonization or at least Lunar Extraction projects sooner or later," said Sue.

"You're not wrong this time! I am glad about skipping a plan or two but doing things step-by-step does feel right sometimes," remarked Lily.

"And because of this mission, we get extra work! Maybe special missions, and hopefully large scale projects! This is all going to be sooo fun to work on!! I have prepared all my notes on Lunar topics for this and my-," began Lucy.

"Oh yes! Good job! We can also show Martina all our hard work! She can check all our work and correct it and we might get a promotion!!" beamed Sue.

"You're right! A promotion would increase our pay and give us the opportunity to participate in even larger scale projects!! Just imagine all the work we could do!" said Lucy.

"And I can make timetables for the entire thing! Wouldn't this be fun! We should defini-," Sue began again.

"Cut it out, you two! We still have to focus on the mission!" snapped Lily. They arrived at their dorm.

"Sue, Lucy, let's have a talk in private with Sam later. Something is clearly not right!" whispered Lily as the dorm came into sight.

"I understand. After shift tomorrow," signalled Lucy.

"I'll text the same on our private server," added Sue.

Sue kept the gear in a drawer. And they began to work on their newly assigned task. The friends did believe that the information Martina had given them was invaluable but could they really trust someone who came out of the blue.

Had they just fallen for a trick? For one, Lily did not trust Martina. I mean she came out of nowhere and said all of this without any hesitation whatsoever. A senior officer would never give away this sort of 'confidential information' right?

She was certain that Martina was just gaslighting them. How could she explain this to Lucy?

Sue meanwhile began to mistrust Lucy. Why was she so supportive of Martina? Could it be past relations or was it something more? Lucy might just be a bit innocent but by now she should know not to trust sketchy people.

Sam meanwhile was certain Martina had something to do with the incident. He was sure that if they could expose her, they would get to know the truth.

Lucy was wondering whom to trust and whether she herself could be trusted. Was I too abrupt in supporting her? What is really going on?

For all they knew, they just had to trust the process for now. Maybe Dr John would be of some help.

Full of all sorts of questions, the friends drifted off to sleep.

The next day, the spacecraft landed on the Moon and they were given all the instructions on work which would begin the following day.

Sue and Lucy were ecstatic. Lily didn't care much about this new development. Sam was also not too fazed about it; mainly after seeing Sue and Lucy's reaction.

X
The Meeting

This day was quite ordinary; they had the job of building bots for farming and repairs.

"I will focus on the hardware and 3D modeling," said Sam packing his things.

"And I'll be making sure you do your work!" said Martina, grabbing her tablet and a notebook.

By 9:00 they all headed out, Martina was wide awake that day. They got to work. Lily was half done by the afternoon. Meanwhile, the others had finished the blueprint and material design.

The blueprint was ready by lunch break and the code was half down.

"How's the work going?" asked Lily as she sat down to eat.

"Well, as smoothly as possible with two workaholics," replied Sam. "Excuse you! We are still here!" argued Sue and Lucy. "Calm down! You want to finish before 6 or not?" asked Lily.

"Yeah, yeah,"

"Sue! I have finished with the blueprint. Can you see if I could add any components?" asked Lucy, passing her a blueprint.

"Hmm... This will need a better control system and lowering mechanism," said Sue as she glanced over and edited the sketch "Sam, you add these to the model before printing."

"You guys will be done soon, right?" asked Lily who had just finished her work.

"What is your speed?" asked Lucy, shocked.

"I am just fast," said Lily proudly. "Yeah, yeah, I beat you once," said Sam. "Yeah, once!" repeated Lily.

After an hour they were done, just in time for their meeting at 6. They quickly headed out.

"We better have the meeting in your room, Lily," said Sam heading towards the room "Martina doesn't enter it for some reason."

"Yeah, sure!" beamed Lily.

"By the way, why doesn't Martina enter your room?" asked Lucy curiously.

"Well, that's a trade secret!" said Lily. Then, headed back to their dorm. After entering Lily's room, they sat down to talk.

"Doesn't anyone think it is suspicious that a senior officer would reveal such 'confidential' information?" asked Lily after checking if the doors were locked properly.

"Yes, but why would she agree to take part in this?" said Sam.

"I don't know but I believe it has something to do with Team SSRS. Why would she know about them when literally no one else did? I asked a few of the teams and they claim to have not heard of these incidents or that they didn't know of Team SSRS at all until now," pointed out Sue

"Also, the suffix 'RS' comes for problematic teams."

"Hmm... Is this a cover-up or something else?" wondered Lucy.

"And Lucy, why did you support Martina?" asked Sue.

"I thought that it could be right. I didn't know that much about the company and stuff like that," explained Lucy "I couldn't understand who was right so..."

"Well, you are not wrong to get confused but I have to ask, did you know Martina before?" asked Lily.

"Yes, she was one of the teachers from one of my extra classes. You may not know her because she wasn't one of your subject teachers. She used to teach history," began Lucy

"She later left the organization. She said she had got a promotion at another branch. But that all seemed odd.

"One day, I asked the front desk person there about her and what exactly happened and he said that she got fired. He said 'Naughty grandma meddling in the company, she was! Got what she deserved, she did! Accused of suspicious activity!' He looked happy in saying this.

"I hoped that I could know why she got fired. I mean what can you do so wrong that you get fired? But I immediately noticed that she had no intention of revealing anything when she came up with all that."

"But if you did know her, why didn't you use that as an advantage to interrogate her?" asked Lily "I mean whatever suspicious activity she might be doing today, she could use you as a cover-up... Hmm, I think you forgot or got too nervous to ask her".

"I am sorry. It seems like I am lying but that didn't come to mind," replied Lucy.

"Well, since they accuse her of 'suspicious' activity, I think it would be crucial to know how and what she taught," suggested Sam.

"You are right, and Lucy, did you like that teacher? And did you find her whereabouts after or before graduating? This could be big! And you should have told us before! Seriously! What did you think we would do?!" exclaimed Sue.

"Shh! She'll hear us and we'll be dead!" interrupted Sam "She is still in the dorm. Keep quiet!" hissed Lily.

"I know for a fact that the history teacher's replacement happened a few months before graduation because you told me that one day," continued Sue.

"That day I just brushed it off as one of your usual class talks. I mean you went to a lot of extra classes."

"Yeah, now I understand why you had to eat rotten food," remarked Lily.

"Hey! I did that to improve my understanding of the world! And I only did that once!" snapped Lucy.

"Well... Lily is kinda right...," said Sam.

"Oh, shut up!" Lucy snapped again.

"Also, was there a change in the way the new teacher taught which was even a little different from hers? Did you ask her why she left the organisation?" asked Sue who was trying to change the subject of the discussion.

"Well, I did try to talk to her but... she left. She said she had work elsewhere and left after looking at her phone," explained Lucy.

"Hmm... work you say? What time did you ask her?" asked Lily.

"And did she leave abruptly?" guessed Sam.

"I asked her when work times were over at 8:30; the maximum work time on the mission schedule," explained Lucy "She did leave as soon as I asked her."

"We'll have to look into it... For now, let's go to bed. A beautiful new day awaits us! And we can do so much more tomorrow!" began Lucy "Right, Sue?"

"Yes! We might also get a building project! Eek!" continued Sue. Both Sue and Lucy burst into a discussion.

"There they go again..." sighed Lily as she shooed them out of the room "By the way, good night!"

"Good night!" Sam wished back as he closed the door, guiding Sue and Lucy out.

XI

A Very 'Uneventful' Day

The next day, they were organising boxes of the newly acquired materials. The friends were in a storage capsule – a large pill looking cylinder into which supplies were loaded to be sent and received from the main base (the Mars Base). Martina had gone somewhere and wasn't there.

On this particular day, they were quite bored and decided to talk for a bit until the next load of materials came in.

"So, about what we discussed yesterday," began Lily after checking if anyone was listening. "Don't you think it's weird that she avoided the question completely? You know, Martina,"

"Yes... I don't know what this could mean as either she is embarrassed – unlikely or she did something," said Sam "She could have found work elsewhere as well, so what's the big deal?"

"Yeah, but I don't think she is telling the truth," said Lucy "She has been teaching for more than 5 years at that organisation. Why would she leave so suddenly it does not make sense!"

"Did she tell you why she left?" asked Sam, intrigued.

"Well... Oh, the rest of the supply's here!" said Lucy as she was interrupted by the arrival of the supplies.

"Is that the last lot?" Lily asked the person who brought the supplies on a sort of miniature truck and was unloading them.

"Yep!" he yelled back "Last for this one!"

"Great, Frank! Keep your truck there, we are coming to get it," Lily yelled back.

"Frank?" asked Lucy, wondering who it was.

"I met him at the lab the other day with Sam. Nice guy, works in the IT department," answered Lily "Today, he had to fill in."

The friends went up to Frank and took the supplies. Frank was a kind but overworked-looking worker with brown hair and a messy attire.

"Hey, got your invigilator yet?" asked Sam "All the teams were getting them."

"Not yet," replied Frank "Good thing too, we are busy enough without any annoying 'supervisors'"

"Right!" said Lily "This is Lucy and Sue – the rest of my team."

"Nice to meet you," said Frank.

"Frank! There is another job, come here!" called out a voice from the distance.

"My teammate, we are substituting today. Gotta go!" said Frank hurrying away.

Just then, Martina entered the capsule – after 15 minutes – holding a cup of coffee.

"Sorry, I need my coffee morning's," said Martina unusually excited "So, have you been good, ay?"

"Yes," groaned Lily, picking a box from the many boxes Frank had delivered.

They all go to work without work after that. Martina left yet again a few minutes later – this time to use the washroom. The friends didn't mind. Martina had already tried to lie to them and evidently not trustworthy.

"Strange, she keeps leaving," said Lucy as she went to get another box "It's as if she is running away,"

"Well, what can we do? She does what she wants," said Lily, drinking some water from her bottle "Anyway, she's annoying."

"Strange isn't it though?" asked Sue.

"Yes, she is plotting something..." said Sam entering passcodes to securely lock the capsule "Look at this, I mean if she is not why would she be so 'busy'? Most invigilators work 24/7, right?"

"Hmm, interesting...," said Lily, sitting down to rest. "That is right; invigilators are supposed to be vigilant. There's something fishy going on."

"Well, we found out. This is definitely not the full picture," said Sue who was also at work.

"I did ask other staff after asking the front desk person and they all seemed to be pleased. As if they had solved all their problems, as if they hated her and were glad that she was gone," said Lucy, putting the last of the things from the boxes in place.

"When I asked about the 'suspicious activity' thing they all said it was a 'dirty little lie'."

"Interesting, Martina has definitely done something to screw them over then," said Sue "I mean people don't say things like that out of the blue."

"We sho-," began Sam, only to be interrupted by Martina entering the room looking very messy and holding what seemed to be a maroon cloak in her right hand and a water bottle in her left.

"Goody! You all are don'! Good job, I'll be busy. You can head back" said Martina before promptly heading out before any of them could say a word.

"Well, someone's preoccupied!" snorted Sam "Come on! We better send this thing and go back. Its pretty late."

The friends headed back to their dorm. After they arrived, they all headed into Lily's room – much to Lily's frustration – and locked the doors.

"Can you not pick a different ROOM?" asked Lily frustratedly.

"Well, yours is the safest...," said Sam.

"Shut up!"

"Anyway, what were we talking about" asked Sue changing the subject "And focus you two!" she snapped at Lily and Sam.

Lily and Sam were in a heated debate on which room was the safest in the dorm and hearing Sue's warning got back to the discussion and stood up.

"Bummer, I had almost won," groaned Lily.

"Truly," groaned Sam.

"This is precisely why you don't get extra marks for your behaviour!" said Sue, annoyed.

"Says the one who got less scores in total despite getting a perfect 20 for behaviour in high school," teased Sam.

"And that one year in middle school," added Lily.

"Can we finally continue, already?!" exclaimed Lucy who was by now very frustrated waiting for the discussion to start.

After hearing this all of them sat down, Lily and Sam on the two chairs that were in the room – one for Lily's coding and research desk and the other for her gaming, Lucy sitting on the bed and Sue pondering about the room.

"Where were we at?" asked Sue trying to look important and finally sitting down on the bed.

"I was going to say something," said Sam "Before I got interrupted."

"What?" asked Sue.

"I have a plan," began Sam. "You know how we can't know what Martina's up to because we are either sleeping or at work, so I have a solution!"

"Let's hear it," said Lily, hoping it would be something interesting.

"We can install surveillance cams which we will take out at the end of term to spy on her," said Sam.

"Good idea!" exclaimed Lucy "But how are we going to do that?"

"Simple, Lily's experimenting things!" replied Sam enthusiastically only to be slapped on the back by Lily who was not amused to say the least.

"Fine, but you better not mess up! I am not 'donating again'," snapped Lily.

"Thank you for being co-operative, for once," said Sue.

"Wow! That's pretty rich to come from you," said Lily "Anyway, it's getting late. We'll set the cameras up tomorrow."

"Sounds good!" said Lucy "Sue, did I tell you about the model of cameras I made in my free time?"

"Nope, let's go check it out!" said Sue. And both of them hurried out of Lily's room.

"Alright, we'll make it when we are not being watched," said Sam.

"Good night," said Lily as she led Sam out.
"Good night!"

XII

The Cameras

That day, everyone got up early – well as early as possible. Sue woke up at 6 and Lucy at 6:15. Sam woke up at 6:30 and Lily woke up at 7.

They all got ready quickly and headed out. Only now, did they start to talk while checking the tasks log.

"We have to check on the food supplies we took with us from the main base and record the data for our first task. Then we need to go and check out some of the mining equipment," Sue read out loud.

"Not much. We'll have time to make the cameras after we are done and then we will have lunch," said Sam "So, we better start working now if we want to finish on time."

"Sure, let's go to the Supply Closet," said Lily "We can get the stuff there."

The Supply Closet was a large room about the size of a warehouse. It was where all supplies, food and equipment was kept for storage and future use.

They headed in and started work. Sam managed to sneak some of the things needed.

XIII

Suspicious Activity

The friends were going about work as usual. Now, Martina had come to ignore them and the questions. She would always either be on a call or going to the restroom during their work sessions. This was happening a lot more and more often.

"What is going on?! Why is Martina acting strangely?" asked Lucy one morning "Any leads?"

"Nope but it seems as though she is planning something with others," said Lily.

"That's right!" said Sue in agreement.

"Well, we got to just wait and watch," said Sam.

"Well then, what about the cams?" asked Sue.

"Let's see," said Lily

They looked into the footage – the first few clips of it to be exact. Martina came into the room wearing a dark maroon cloak with a mysterious symbol on it – it was 12:00 AM.

"Why is Martina coming back here late at night every single time? Is this not a clue?" said Lily.

"She is also wearing a weird maroon cloak – one with the symbol on the back. What do you reckon?" asked Sam.

"The symbol... From what I know at least, it looks like a symbol some cult might use," said Sue.

"I... have seen that symbol before...," said Lucy looking as though she had been struck by a flashback.

"Where?" jumped Sam.

"Well, it was during one of Martina's classes. She started with the topic of fates people wish to follow. While explaining, don't know how, but she came to the subject of the right fate which is where she mentioned... what was it? Oh yes! The fate of Harrison!" said Lucy.

"Interesting... Fate, very reminiscent of cults introduction. Lately – before the big boom! – I had read an article about a cult whose members were arrested. Got what they deserved! That cult – the infamous Pristine Truth! They had revealed some of their practices of indoctrination." Began Lily

"The first of which included the introduction of a fate!"

"Well, any other clues?" asked Sue.

"She is speaking in an unknown language. Also, a classic of cults nowadays," said Lily "They sure are getting creative".

"Interesting! If Martina had joined the cult back when we're in college, the cult ought to be at least 10 years old and also a major party would try and take over a big reputed organisation, am I right?" said Sam.

"I guess. In those days, Martina used to say 'Our leader, a great, great woman, found us the right fate! In her early twenties! Extraordinary! By now o' cours' she's a lil older actually I reckon 45,' I remember her saying this," said Lucy imitating Martina's voice as much as she can.

"Well, you're right then," said Lily with a giggle now realizing that Martina's voice sounded quite funny.

"See!" said Sam.

They continued to review the footage.

One day – they didn't know which at this point – they saw Martina bursting into the main lounge, carrying many files, and talking on the phone in the same undecipherable dialect while hurrying to take off the same cloak.

Sam managed to hear her mentioning a specific date – 21st of August. It was very next day!

"Did you catch that?" beamed Sam "She said in... what was it? Some language... I forgot what it is called. But she said something about the 21st of August – tomorrow,"

"Tomorrow, ay, well, rest assured that we will have quite the day!" said Lily trying to hide her intrigue.

"Yeah, especially you!" teased Sam.

"Hey you...!" snapped Lily.

"I guess we just have to wait and watch. Don't get too excited it might not happen tomorrow," said Sue.

"Bummer!" said Sam sluggishly.

"Aw..." said Lucy, disappointed.

"Buzzkill!" said Lily.

"I am being practical!" said Sue "And that is what one must do to achieve!"

"You're right!" beamed Lucy.

"Now then, it is pretty late. Let's go to bed," said Lily checking the time.

"Yeah sure!" said Lucy. They all went to bed that day, each having different hopes for the coming day. Little did they know that Sue was wrong and something drastic would occur. Well at least, some of them. Lucy was so excited, she couldn't sleep.

Lily was reviewing the footage but eventually fell asleep. Lucy however fell asleep right before 5 AM.

XIV

The Incident...

On the next day, Lily was up just an hour after Sue (she normally wakes up 2 hours later). "Lily, I know it is an anticipated date but how?" said Sue.

"Well, I don't always feel tired," said Lily, looking energetic and brewing a coffee.

"That's good, you are finally learning how to be responsible," said Sue.

"Oh, come on!" snapped Lily. Just then, Lucy burst out of her room, fully dressed and ready for work.

"Good morning! Also, Sue, I was awake before you; so I won the bet and secondly, I took a look at the symbol on Martina's cloak before bed!" she exclaimed.

"Well, here's the cash and good job!" said Sue handing over some cash "Oh yeah, we set a bet after you and Sam went to bed,"

Sam came in a few minutes later. They had breakfast in their room and headed out. Sue checked the tasks log.

"Today we have to go out and look for hazardous patches since the other team specialised or trained in that field is out of commission... strange," said Martina who had joined them minutes after they headed out "Moving on, we've gotta register the data in to the resource folder and that's about it!"

"Hazardous what?" asked Lucy.

"Hazardous patches like deep craters, radioactive or dangerous regions," explained Martina.

"Well, we'll head out then," said Sam, taking the lead.

"Yeah," said Lily, following him.

"I won't be there'... um... I have some work elsewhere," said Martina, trying to get away from them.

Sam and Lily stopped in their tracks. "What?!" they both said, shocked and at the same time.

"Yes, it's importan' gotta go!" said Martina hurrying off, away from them before any of them could say a thing.

"What just happened?" said Lucy, confused.

"I don't know whether this is a good or bad omen," said Lily.

"Why would she be leaving work? Invigilators are supposed to watch their teams – especially if they are going out! The incident that led to the whole thing happened on an outdoor mission," said Sue.

"Welp, we can't get to her now because she has apparently disappeared," said Lily.

"Let's just get to work. Anyway, we only have to work on a few metres. It should be done in a few hours," said Sam shrugging off the matter and going to get his suit.

"Sure," sighed Sue as she and the others followed.

They put on their suits quickly and headed out.

After a few hours, they were done. They went to change, came back now in their normal attire and headed out into the hallway leading to the tech lab to register the data when...

A woman – an old one who would be about the same age as the leader Martina had mentioned to Lucy – came rushing in. She was wearing a maroon cloak with a strange symbol on the back which the friends reckoned to be the same as the one Martina was wearing.

"RUN! RUN, RUN, RUN! Terrible things are to happen! There is a blaze from the sun coming towards us!" she yelled, bringing everyone in the area to a halt.

"Yes... yes. Very unfortunate," chimed a sizable crowd behind her wearing the same outfit. There were 10 people standing just behind her, one of them having the same hair colour and appearance as Martina.

"Lets give up on this mission! For if you want to SURVIVE, you will need to RUN!" she exclaimed with all her might.

"Yes, yes. Oh yes," chimed the crowd in a dreamy tone. There were about 20 of them clearly in sight behind the 10 standing just behind the woman. As the end of the corridor (a heavy metal door leading to the room of records – a place with large hard drives and stuff like that which stored important information) was dimly lit that day, there could be many more of them.

The friends stood there, in confusion, fear and uncertainty. What had just happened? What did this mean?

"So, I was... right! But what does... this mean?" Sam whispered, barely hiding the panic in his voice.

Meanwhile, Lily was intrigued, wanting to know more about the woman before them. "She must be the leader! Let's see her next move." Lily thought out loud.

"Ssh! So, she is the infamous leader," whispered Sue.

"It's definitely her!" said Lucy as quietly as she could.

The woman continued "COME WITH US! To a place where these dangers cannot hurt you, YOU ALL!"

"Come with us! Come with us!" chimed the others.

"Um Sam, you better go call Dr John before the whole place is on their side. They seem convincing," Lily whispered to Sam urging him to go and tell Dr John.

"Got it!"

Sam slowly began to get away from the crowd. Many of them were looking on in horror and with hope. They were – to the terror of the friends, who were now hoping that at least some of their fellow researchers were to stand up and do something about this obvious attempt to indoctrinate – in a trance.

They looked at the crowd before them and their leader with hope.

Sam, after hurrying away from the crowd, rushed to Dr John's office.

"Sir! There is a problem, a big one in the hall near the room of records! There is mass clad in maroon," said Sam panting as he entered.

"Clad in maroon! Take me there and carry a mic," instructed Dr John the moment he heard the words 'clad in maroon' as if he knew what had happened.

They rushed to the hall. Sam set up the mic and handed it to Dr John.

"Everybody, keep calm! And… you," said Dr John on the mic "You stay put! We need to verify your Claims."

"WHAT'S THERE TO 'claim'?! A lot of us could very well die!" she yelled back.

"You are making a mistake! A grave mistake!" chimed the crowd behind her.

"Since there is no evidence to support your 'claim'. We need to test it, don't we?" said Dr John "You very well know, we have every reason not to trust you."

"You MAY NOT for your idiocy... But WE and NOW THEY KNOW BETTER," she yelled.

"Do you seriously think you can deceive us again?" said Dr John who was very much restraining from using force "I ask again, what are you trying to pull?"

"Trying to pull! I am trying to save your LIVES!" she exclaimed, facing Dr John, looking almost like someone who'd been seen through before she faced the crowd dressed in maroon and said "See this! The ones who vow to tell the truth are always overstepped!"

They all nodded as though in a trance.

"Hey- let me jus-. Dr John what is going on? And what were you talking about?" asked Lily who came pushing through the crowd.

"Yes, let us through, will you?" said Sam as he and Lucy jostled behind Lily.

They seemed to be the only ones who were not buying the woman's act.

"Well, we shall have a talk about this another day," replied Dr John who noticed this "For now, help me get the situation under control. Lily, you call security from the security and defence department 2nd floor 3rd base,"

"Yes..." agreed Lily, dashing off.

"So, you are going to call the security on me. SEE THIS! THEY ARE ALL LIARS!!" she exclaimed loudly.

This continued and the woman and her 'followers' started a sort of divide among the staff, all of whom had gathered at the spot. The friends stayed on the left of the woman and her followers beside Dr John.

Lily came running back with the security units.

"Sir, sorry for the late arrival. Too many people were coming to see what the commotion was about," said Lily.

"It is alright. You are on time... Not many of them have defected yet," said Dr John "Security contains them!"

The security unit, while small, was very effective. They managed to get the now defected (to the woman's side) and the main culprits under control – separating them and taking them away to containment areas (which were built for emergencies for the storage of hazardous substances and dangerous staff).

The unit did all this as if knowing what to do – as if it had happened before.

"Please make your way back to your dorms and all work is cancelled for the day as we need to verify the claims and control the situation," said Dr John handing the mic over to Sam and signalling for him to keep it in his office.

Sam rushed up to Dr John's office and the others headed to their dorm.

"What was that all about?" asked Lily.

"I don't know but it looks like Dr John is not quite fond of the woman," said Sam.

XV

Work As Usual Or So We THOUGHT!

The day after the incident, since the revolutionaries – the ones who sided with the woman – were put under temporary containment. Work continued as usual.

The friends went on to do everyday tasks and some aspects of the mission were put on hold until the issue was resolved.

Martina was still their invigilator due to lack of replacements. She now didn't live with the friends, she stayed with the other rebels. She would come take a look at their work and leave at the end of the working day.

The Moon base was finally fully set up and research on the 'impending solar flare' continued. Dr John was able to direct his attention away from the effects of the incident after the discovery of a large deposit.

The woman was put in a secluded section of the base. She was to be interrogated when they got back. The newly discovered deposit has greatly helped the mission give results. And because of this, the teams are getting more and more outdoor projects and tasks.

Team SSTR is working on a mine at the site of the discovery and are at the moment too preoccupied to look into the suspicious activity.

"Sam, don't you think this is a good opportunity to just relax!" said Sue through the intercom.

"Yeah, but these new projects are tiring!" said Sam.

"Sue, Lily, let's have a talk later," suggested Lucy.

They all agreed. Later in the evening, they met up at Lily's room.

"So, what do you want to talk about?" asked Sue "If it about work studi-,"

"No, it's about what has happened over the days before!" said Lucy "What do you guys even want to do?"

"Well, Me and Lily are looking through the matter with the intention of investigating the whole story," said Sam.

"That will definitely give answers to almost all the queries we might have," added Lily "Lucy, do you notice anything about the day of the incident that is strange?"

"Well, yes. That woman was speaking in the same way Martina used to. She started screaming at the thought of acting in a normal and polite manner.

She refused to be confronted with facts. This is too similar to what Martina used to do. Wait! How could I forget?!

After Martina left, some of the other students also went missing from class. After that, some of the students were also expelled," said Lucy.

"Sue, any thoughts?" asked Sam.

"Yes! This is the same as what happened the other day," said Sue, "Many of the staff were suspended and that includes Martina. So, this proves that Martina has something to do with the incident!"

"So, who's in on investigating this together?" asked Sam.

The others agreed. They decided to ask Dr John about what had happened and if he knew something they didn't.

So, the next day, they decided to ask him once they were done with work.

"Hmm... What tasks do we have today?" said Sue as she packed up her things for work.

Sue scanned through the tasks.

"We have to look at the new mining site and register the data. And there is an email from Dr John,"

The friends gathered around Sue to read the email. The email read:

Team SSTR,

I am assigning you an extra task which is confidential. You need to sort files on **The Cult of Harrison**. Also, for this task you will not be accompanied by your invigilator, Martina Goodwill. Kindly keep all the information confidential

After doing the above, meet me at my office with the files and we will have a discussion on the topic.

Regards

Dr John

In-charge of term 1 of Mission Moonscape

Dr.John's Email

"Well, this is lucky," remarked Sam.

"Yes! And judging from the day of the incident, Dr John definitely knows something!" said Lucy.

"So, this is quite the opportunity!" beamed Sue and Lily (at the same time). After doing so, they stared at each other with looks expressing 'how on earth did you think and say the same thing as me' then Sam and Lucy and then faced opposite directions at the walls on either side. They then avoided eye-contact and there was an awkward silence.

Sam burst out laughing after much restraint "I guess opposites – oh sorry – best friends think alike!"

Hearing this, Lucy too burst into peals of laughter.

"Are you seriously laughing?!" snapped Sue "It is quite immature. People think the same thing sometimes. It is perfectly normal!"

"Not for you two," giggled Lucy.

"Whatever! Let's get to work," said Lily storming off "And Sue, good job on getting smarter to think like me," she said as she paused to grab her backpack - leaning beside the door at the start of the narrow corridor leading to their dorm - and open the door.

"Smarter?! You should be thankful!" snapped Sue grabbing her things and hurrying out too.

"Here we go," sighed Sam and Lucy as they too headed out.

At the IT department, they got to work on their computers. The IT department of this base was near the mining fields and solar panels.

All the files they found on the Cult of Harrison, they had some text that was censored. They tried many ways to access it but it didn't work.

XVI

The End of Mission Moonscape's 1st Term

It was a day before the end of their term on the Moon Base. Lily, Sue, Sam and Lucy received emails detailing all the conditions. The email (the same one was sent to all of them) described the following:

Greetings!

As you have been notified the day before, you have to follow certain conditions to proceed with the mission. They are listed as follows:

> You are not permitted to let anyone know of this mission.
> Your personal emails are blocked for the time being to prevent information leaks through hacking

> You are under obligation to tell Dr Jones and Smith about the matter along with myself

> Your regular duties will be paused.

If you agree to said conditions, reply yes.

Regards,

Dr John.

Dr. John's Email

Sue quickly and enthusiastically read through the terms. Lily got out of bed sluggishly and turned on the room's internal heating.

When she did so, the virtual holograph disappeared for a split second before displaying the following message which was read aloud by an automated voice.

YOU ARE ALREADY TOO LATE! YOU HAVE BEEN FOOLED.

ALL YOUR 'PREDICTIONS' ARE WRONG! YOU HAVE BEEN FOOLED. IT IS NOT TOO LATE TO JOIN OUR SIDE…

The Automated Voice Message

By the time the message ended, everyone was at the scene except Martina.

"What does this... mean?" said Lily frantically.

"So, we were wrong after all. But about what?" asked Sue looking just as shocked as Lily.

"I... I don't know," stammered Sam.

"Wait! All that we thought was wrong?! Then what is going on?" thought out loud Lucy.

"We don't know but we must inform Dr John now!" exclaimed Sue hurrying off still half dressed, only having her shirt and tie on – her coat lying in her room.

They rushed through corridors looking as though they had been late for work and had dressed as shabbily as they could.

They arrived after a while at Dr John's office.

"Sir! You need to see this!" said Sue barging in.

"What is it? And why are you all dressed... like this?" asked Dr John, less concerned than confused.

"Look, sir, we are sorry for arriving at this get-up but, you need to hear this," said Lily.

"What?" he asked.

They explained the whole incident to him.

"Oh really. Stooped this low... And we didn't get a hint of it," Dr John murmured to himself as though he had known of such incidents.

"What do you mean?" asked Sam.

"You'll understand in a bit. The truth is, this has happened before, though much differently from now. Back then, it was a rivalry now it is a full-on battle. They have tried this just a few years before you all joined," began Dr John.

"What do you mean this has happened before? If it has, then why are they still here?" asked Lily.

"Yeah, and why aren't they locked up or something?" asked Sue.

"And about the message, did they know what we were talking about?" asked Lily.

"Yes..." replied Dr John "If you can share with me the object of your discussions, I can clear things up."

The friends explained all their discussions.

"Your predictions are spot on! You even learnt of the cult's name! Bravo! But there is one issue... You were too late to find out," said Dr John.

"What do you mean too late?" asked Sam.

"Well, this has happened before... So, I would know. Back then it started much differently than now, "It has happened before we had stopped allying with 'the cult'. Or should I say rival organisation," began Dr John

"It all started when we first started out about 20 years ago. I was there about 4 and a half years after it started. The organisation at the time was partnered with two investors. One of the GOVT Foundation of Science and Research which was still supporting us even before the incident – the one with the powerplant thing.

"And the other was the Cult of Harrison. They were more secretive and – I don't know if this is true – it was rumoured that Dr Jones and Smith had known the cult's leader since they were very young. Some say that this is why they were investing in SCI.CORP.

"The cult had initially supported us – a lot in fact! But something changed, the leader not content in sharing our profits, soon began demanding sectors of the company – we complied thinking that they need the sectors for their own commercial development. Back then, we had the historical and archaeological departments for context.

"Dr Jones and Smith agreed to hand them over as the cult's contributions were still substantial at the time. "After attaining the departments however, their funding slowly decreased and they withdrew their alliance with the company a year later. Ever since, they have been funding rival projects and attempting to frame the company.

"And what did they do to the departments? They made them into new organisations to promote historical research and also their cult.

"Oh yes and the people's cloaks you mentioned. They were the cult... They had snuck in after pulling a 'prank'. They were let in by the new guards after blackmailing them – she was among them.

"I assume, Martina told you something about that,"

"Yes, Martina did tell us this. That the people who snuck in were traitors ruining the organisation's reputation," said Sam "So, was she right?"

"Yes, partly. She was telling the truth, partly but she was not speaking from the right perspective. She, the leader and the other cult members, were the ones who snuck in. They knew of the explosion and ran for shelter," said Dr John "She didn't tell you – of course."

"There was 'resistance'?" asked Lily.

"Well, yes. Laur... I mean the leader instigated this. As you have described your investigations, the same results were found at first but they seemed to be wrong," replied Dr John.

"Who did you say?" asked Sam "Laurina, Laurenda... Laurea, Laura, Lauren?"

"Look, that is not im-,"

"How is it not? If we know her or him, we can solve this right?" asked Lucy.

"I will tell you..."

"Ok, but what did that message mean?" asked Lily.

"It MEANT that they had already done something big! And the incident was Phase One!"

"Well, what should we do now?" asked Sam.

"From now onwards, I will give you a few tasks and a folder. For those, you simply need to do it while collecting info. You need to interrogate the woman in the meantime and here are some folders on the topic for you to reference for the above,"

"Alright!" they all beamed as they headed out half in excitement and half in uncertainty.

"We should get to work then!" said Sue, looking as though nothing had happened.

"Sure!" beamed Lucy who also became engrossed in the folders.

And so, they got to work. Everyday, from start to end of Mission Moonscape. They collectively stored their information in a shared folder to present to Dr John when he called for that.

As their term on the Moonscape base came to an end, Dr John and the rest of the Teams involved began preparations for the next group's term.

Dr John called them to a talk later on the evening of their last day at the base. The friends entered his office.

"So, since the mission is coming to an end and Martina had been put under control and would be getting a separate compartment in the rocket along with the others.

So, you guys have done the work I presume," said Dr John.

"Yes!" beamed Sue and Lucy.

They began to present.

"Evidence suggests that they indeed were framing the company in the previous incidents but not for the reason Martina gave.

They appeared to have had a group of their own in the field of scientific research. We got this from some facts that tied the thing together," said Lily "That is the most important."

"Interesting! Have you found out about any individuals in particular?" asked Dr John.

"Well, no matter where we look, we always come across the name Lauren Stranford," said Lucy "Martina had mentioned someone going by that name before."

"Did she say anything about her?"

"Yes, she said that she was some leader," said Lucy.

"Leader... Well, you are spot on at that. She is the leader but before I will elaborate on some topics. Firstly, our objective in finding out more about them is to solve some mysteries they left behind. And for this mission it is to stop their plan which is to take over SCI.CORP.

We need to stop their influence – God knows what will happen this time. Let me just say, the last time was the worst of it.

We have seen from past experiences that they are not going to do any good. Also, on the topic, Team SSRS was their main look out for performing rituals that benefit only them in return.

So, our objective is to isolate the cult before their plans have been fully enacted," explained Dr John.

"But we are leaving the base today and just what will we tell Dr John and Smith?" asked Sam.

"Well, the answer to that is complicated and I will find out and let you know. Meanwhile, you can help the others take the woman from her quarters on the spaceship and also try and 'talk' to her," said Dr John, ushering them out.

"Alright!" they said heading out.

"Well, aren't we lucky?" said Sue.

"We know more about the mystery and now we get to talk to her!" said Lucy.

"I have to admit I did not expect it to be so simple," said Lily as they headed out.

They walked past many of the bases and then finally arrived at their location. There they saw the same woman, now dressed in a grey frock.

She was in a room reminiscent of a hotel room. It had a basic double bed dressed with starched white sheets. The room was well lit with a bedside table (about the size of a stool), a desk and chair with a pen, paper and a table lamp.

She had the same greying hair and furrowed at the friends – recognising them from the incident.

"What do you want?" she barked at them getting up from her desk.

"Could we have a 'talk'?" asked Lily signalling the security to head out and lock the door behind them.

"What is your name?" asked Lucy.

"Why do you want TO KNOW?!" she said slyly "You still don't get it? Good! Anyway, what do you want to 'talk' about?"

"Well, let us start off simple. Intentions!" said Sue.

"We all have them – some open, some hidden," continued Sam "So, will you tell us yours?"

"Why did you do what you did?" asked Lucy.

"Why should I?"

"It is a shame you won't tell us?" said Lily "Oh come on, what will you lose?"

"Shut up!" the woman threw the lamp at them. The lamp went flying, it nearly hit both Sue and Lily who were standing close together – they stepped away, then, went towards Lucy in a sort of right angle like path – she ducked and then finally Sam caught it.

"No need to get violent! Just tell us and... we will leave," said Sam.

"Fine then!" she said as the security unit outside flinched and prepared to attack "Let's just say my intention is to conquer the opponent and finally bring some sense into the fools,"

"Talking in riddles... Anyway, we have one last question," said Lily "How far have you gone in accomplishing your goal? In fulfilling your goal?"

She stared unwillingly, then attempted to throw the chair before the security threatened to enter.

"Fine, fine!" she scowled "No use in fighting back... So, let's just say I completed Phase One."

"Very well, what do you mean?" asked Sue.

"That is up to you to interpret. I can't be lying right?" she said.

"Well played..." said Lily who was sure she was hiding something.

The friends headed back to their dorm to get some things.

"Wow! Rude!" exclaimed Lily slamming the door closed.

"I know! We only wanted to talk jeez!" said Sam, irritated by the woman's antics.

"I just realized, we never got to know her name. Dr John had almost mentioned it but stopped," said Lucy.

"Curious..." said Sue packing her backpack.

"We better ask him today. It's our last day on the Moon," said Lily, picking up her things and opening the door.

They agreed and headed out. After a few minutes, they arrived at Dr John's office, where he was giving instructions to load the extracted materials onto the ships that were going to take the term back to the base.

"Oh yes," said Dr John, noticing them "What did you find out?"

"Well, we asked her a few questions but let's just say, she did not appreciate the questioning," said Sam.

"She threw a lamp at me and Sue and you're saying she just did not appreciate it," said Lily.

"Expected," said Dr John, unsurprised as though he had seen this before "So, what did you find out?"

"Well, she did not exactly tell us anything straight up and got violent... So, we didn't get to know much," said Lucy.

"Then, tell me what she did say," said Dr John.

The friends told him everything she had said. There was a long pause after that.

"We're definitely too late! Darn!" muttered Dr John "Follow me, I need to look at something. It's important."

The friends followed Dr John without a word wondering what he was talking about.

XVII

The Last Time

They headed to wherever they were going in silence.

"Where are we going?" asked Sue jogging to keep up with Dr John who was walking very quickly.

"The records room,"

"For what?" asked Sam.

"You'll see,"

They got into the records room. A large library-like room where there were disks – large paper sized short boxes which had a hole to plug a wire into – and all sorts of other storage devices. It had multiple rows and two columns with a few desktops on a round table in the space between the columns.

Each of the rows were labelled based on what information their hard drives contained.

It was about the size of a library. It had a large monitor screen at the back which had its own controls. This is the first time the friends have ever seen such a place.

"You know how I said this has happened before. Well, it was pretty ugly. You need to know what happened then to know what to expect," said Dr John walking over to a row in the first column labelled 'CLT101'. He took out a heavy looking drive and walked over to the monitor and plugged a wire in.

Then, on the screen, appeared a series of files like the ones on computer screens. Dr John sighed then finally spoke.

"Well, I have been telling you again and again that this sort of thing had happened before but... judging by what she said you definitely need to know what happened before.

"I will tell Dr Jones and Smith that you will also be helping with the effort but you'll need to know what to expect."

"What do you mean 'the effort'? Is that a secret mission?" asked Sue enthusiastically.

"No, it's a sector. I know I am not supposed to reveal any of this but with what you have found out with your limited time with Martina could be important," said Dr John "This sector handles all the stuff related to this. It is to be dissolved when the problem is solved but there was always the possibility of it happening again. I don't know when this sector will be dissolved but it's not anytime soon."

"So, from what I can guess, you are saying that the last time they attacked they did something so bad that there was an entire sector there just to fight them?" said Sam.

"That's right," said Dr John.

"So, what exactly happened?" asked Lily "I mean you told us already right?"

"This is the reason why we are trying to isolate the Cult of Harrison." said Dr John. "And no, we are not trying to wage war. This is a means to coexist."

The whole room went silent. Nobody spoke a word, everyone intrigued.

"The last time we thought the cult was just another money hungry organisation," began Dr John "But, we couldn't be more wrong,"

Dr John clicked on the folder labelled 'The People of Harrison'. The friends wondered what this meant. Were the People of Harrison a cult? A new species? What were they?

"Well, I can see you are a little confused." said Dr John.

"Yeah, well, if you come up to us with an almost fictitious name, we will have questions." said Lily.

"Yeah, and there is no such word in the dictionary," said Sue who was now holding a large dictionary.

"That is exactly what was so disturbing and why there was a special sector... The Harrisonians or People of Harrison - they were discovered about 5 years ago. They are an alien race and they are allied with the cult.

"We discovered them when we were just about to get the cult under control after a legal talk, we were heading out to negotiate. Lauren was not cooperative, one of her followers was with her and she whispered something to her and she said something very loudly.

"It was something we couldn't understand like a different language she was speaking to what looked like a strange microphone. Just then, there was a green light covering the sky." said Dr John showing a blurry picture.

"A ship – clearly a spaceship appeared on the horizon and started blasting lasers at us – we were near the research base – and we ducked inside a shed nearby. "Then, a peculiar figure levitated down from the ship through a green beam of light. The figure was humanoid, having short legs and tentacles like those of an octopus covering its mouth. It looked aged with wrinkles all over its bald head. It was wearing what looked to be a long black coat being dragged on the ground.

"I think it was a distinct hue of maroon, its face resembling a very old man. With what could be seen of the creature's eyes through its wrinkles and eyelids, they were pitch black. A peculiar sight indeed

"Then, it said something in the same language as Lauren. One of my colleagues was there with me, Dr Jones and Dr Smith and he had recorded what they had said.

"The ship blasted off across the horizon after levitating the strange fellow back on. All we know is that this was a warning from what it seemed. As after all this happened, Lauren smirked and walked away with her follower.

"We looked into the recording and all we could find out was that they were from a faraway place. Knowing that the cult has access to an alliance with what can be a civilization in space, it is to our best interest if we keep them isolated.

"After that if you are wondering, why is it such a big deal? You need to see what scenes they recreated in hallways every day! Just like what happened on the day of the incident," concluded Dr John.

"Well, that explains a lot but how did they do this in the first place, you know the whole alien thing," said Lily.

"That is unclear. It said to be related to their takeover,"

"No wonder they acted all powerful. They could just call up some aliens to destroy our base, anytime," said Sam, a bit annoyed at Lauren's behaviour from that day.

"Well, that's all I can tell you now. We are leaving the Moon base tomorrow at 10. It's getting late. You all go to bed," said Dr John, switching off the monitor.

"Alright!"

They headed back.

"I completely forgot we were leaving tomorrow!" sighed Lily "Now, I have to pack everything up!"

"You didn't?!" exclaimed Sue looking shocked.

"Here we go again," sighed Sam and both Sue and Lucy began to babble about being responsible workers.

They all went to bed wondering what would happen next.

XVIII
The Departure

The next day, everyone was up early - well nearly everyone. Lily woke up late after spending the night packing up. Team SSTR was working on getting capsules of the last materials harvested onto the spacecraft.

"Why do we have to do all this heavy lifting?" complained Lily as she finally got one on to a loading staircase which was like the staircases that are used to exit planes but with the same mechanism as an escalator.

"It's not that much work. We only have five more to go," said Sue "Not my fault, someone forgot to pack."

"Why you-"

"Calm down! It's like 7 in the morning! Give me a break!" sighed Sam.

They finished doing their job half an hour later and were relaxing on a few boxes that were yet to be loaded.

"The last days are always the worst! God, we still have so much to do!" sighed Lily.

"Well, it's kind of your fault for not packing," said Sue "And anyway, more work is good news! I am getting bored."

"Bored?! We got a break after so long!" said Sam, staring at Sue as if she was something weird.

"Me too. We should get more!" Lucy chimed in.

Sam and Lily both stared and Sue and Lucy for a long time with a look of 'are you two okay'.

"Team SSTR! You all need to go and check if the settings for the launch are correct and stop lounging around!"

"Jeez, we just sat down for a minute!" Lily yelled back.

"Get to work!"

"Fine, fine,"

Team SSTR got to work on their task. Meanwhile the traitors (supporters of the cult) were boarding the ship - followed by many researchers into their separate cabin. Which had full-time surveillance.

After a few hours, everything and everyone was ready to board and for the departure. Sam had gone,

Researchers were now boarding the spacecraft. Sam and Lily sighed a breath of relief; Sue and Lucy had finally stopped lecturing them on the right way to plan out their day.

The boarding took about half an hour. The friends took their seats.

"Whew! Finally, I can sleep," said Lily, looking happier than she had a few minutes ago.

The spacecraft took off a few minutes later. Most of the rest of the flight was uneventful. Except of course, of the occasional lecture from Sue on various topics of discussion.

"You know, we should check the footage. I mean we are allowed to have some privacy now," said Sam, hinting at the curtains that were beside him, attached to the top of his seat and the seat in front of him.

"Sure, it has been a while since we have taken off," said Lucy.

Sam closed the curtains. Lily took out a pen drive which stored the footage from the cameras they had put in it. She took out her laptop, turned it on and plugged the pen drive in.

"This is the footage a day after the incident. The cameras weren't working on the day of the incident. Strange... Martina might have figured us out. I changed their positions that night so the angle will be different," explained Lily.

"Well no wonder, we did ask her a lot of questions," said Lucy, thoughtfully.

"But, on the other hand she might have found out about them on her own," said Sue.

"Both options are possible," said Sam "The fact that she reacted and messed with the cameras instead of confronting us proves that she was doing something wrong. Or else it would not make sense to react that way."

"So, let's check out the footage before we land," said Sue.

"Alright!" said Lily, playing the footage.

On the day after the incident, Martina rushed into the dorm followed by some people who looked like guards that stood by the door. She stormed into her room and hurried out a moment later, carrying one medium-sized bag which was on her suitcase and one suitcase with her cloak stuffed hurriedly into the handbag she was holding in her arm.

One of the people by the door told her to hurry up and pack all her things before anyone woke up. Then Martina yelled at them on how they were inconsiderate for a whole five minutes - which on Lily's part was entertaining to watch.

After an entire hour of Martina, the people by the door told her to pack up another day as they heard Sue and Lucy wake up. Martina called them names under her breath and left with them.

"Well now, we know why she was missing for the last couple of days," said Lucy.

"She wasn't there?" said Lily, sounding astonished.

"Yeah, I thought she just left early in the mornings when you and Sue were awake," said Sam.

"Um, if you all haven't noticed she wasn't there for the entire time after the incident," said Lucy.

They all - including Sue - stared at Lucy with a look of 'wait, you noticed?'.

"Well, now that is surprising, Sue didn't notice a thing!" said Sam.

"Well, it's no wonder," said Sue, sounding a bit annoyed. "She always left a sticky-note when she left early and judging by the fact that she was not present for most of the mission, anyone can forget her."

"It's good she's gone," said Lily "She is so annoying!"

"Wow! Can we please get back to the topic!" said Sue, now irritated.

"Fine," groaned Lily.

Then they discussed the footage. And Sue and Lily got into a heated debate on if what Martina had called the supposed guards was funny.

"Blockhead was a fitting description," said Lily.

"For the fourth time, that's not polite," said Sue.

After that, they decided to continue with the footage later and enjoy the flight.

XIX

Back to Mars

After a day, the spacecraft prepared to land on Mars. The friends were now getting ready to get off.

"Well, that was quick! Did they modify the spacecraft?" asked Lily.

"They did," said Sue.

"We will be landing soon, please remain seated and buckled in," came an announcement through a speaker which was taped to one side of the wall.

The friends sat down and another announcement came from the speaker.

"The boarding order will be as follows; please listen carefully. These instructions will not be repeated. The participants and supporters will be taken out first followed by the security.

"No one is to interupt with this procedure at any cost. Next the SS teams will leave the premises followed . After them the regular maintenance and storage management

"Please follow this order of events for convenience,"

"Well. We better hurry! And you better not snitch!" a suspiciously cautious guard whispered to a researcher who was also strangely cautious and excited.

"This is not right," the researcher whispered back to the guard in a warning tone "If they find out, we're both dead! Come on!"

"Yes… Now, keep your mouth shut will you!" said the guard, sounding nervous "You have the passcode, don't you? You better!" he barked.

"O- of course!" the researcher said in a frightened and nervous tone.

The two of them strolled past Team SSTR and the other SS teams. Walking as nonchalantly as they could to avoid suspicion. The researcher looked scared while the guard looked cautious.

`As they walked past Team SSTR, Sue, Sam, Lily and Lucy all looked at them with suspicion - "is it time to get off already?" asked Lily as she observed carefully "We have an o- order!" the researcher said quickly after the guard glared at him in a frightened tone.

The researcher looked at them longingly as though trying to get away for a few seconds before being dragged away by the guard by force.

As they passed, Lily could have sworn she had seen one of them before. Was it Frank?

Seeing this, the two of them hurried off.

The friends stared at them alone hurrying away. Most of the staff didn't care at all - "Just the usual" they thought.

"What's up with them?" asked Sam, a little annoyed as they - while running - had woken him up.

"Don't know," said Sue who was reading a book. "They seem to be in a hurry."

"Something's fishy," said Lucy.

"Right, I don't think anyone was supposed to move yet," said Lily "We didn't get another announcement,"

"Alright, everyone? Good!" it was Dr John "We will be landing now. Kindly remain seated."

The landing ended fairly quickly and there seemed to be no problems... yet.

Just as they prepared to take the cult out and to their new living quarters, BANG! There was a loud rumble. The spacecraft went unsteady as one of its landing pads (a stub with its tip lit on fire to slow down the fall) had partially broken down.

The landing equipment began to malfunction. The spacecraft tilted side-to-side and finally after many alarms came to a halt and crashed on to Mars from 10 feet above.

The landing pad now broke down completely, its supporting leg fully collapsed, leaving the spacecraft supported only by the ground on one of its sides after it swayed and fell to the ground. Everyone was in shock, nobody said a word and there was brief silence. Then, the beep of an emergency signal from the cockpit of the spacecraft.

Only then, did someone say a word - it was an announcement.

"Please remain seated until the problem is solved. Everyone

"What the heck happened?" said Sam, who was thoroughly surprised.

"Isn't it obvious? Something went wrong," said Lily.

"Could 'they' have something to do with it?" asked Lucy.

"Definitely!" exclaimed Sue, "Did you see how they were walking? They definitely were up to no good,"

"Yeah!" said Sam "They were in such a rush out of the blue and then this happened."

"Right... after we suspected them," beamed Lily "They must have had something to do with what happened now.

Any theories?"

"Well," said Sam "Obviously, the cult members will be the first to leave the spacecraft which could explain why they left before the landing. They were planning something for or related to the cult.

"I suggest that, they somehow didn't want the cult to exit before for whatever reason so, they messed up the landing pad,"

"Likely, but-," began Sue. She was then cut off by an announcement.

"Please remain in place! The cult's enclosure has been broken into. They have escaped. We are investigating the predicament and the perpetrators. We will give updates."

"Rude!" exclaimed Sue, unpleased by the interruption.

"Wait," said Lily, suddenly "Could they be trying to free the cult?"

"That is probable," said Sue, thoughtfully.

After an hour or so, everything had settled - almost. The culprits had not been caught yet and the cult had escaped and were on the loose. The spacecraft's landing pad however was being repaired. The friends had gotten off and moved into their dorm.

Most of the staff found the incident a nuisance - complaining all the way to their dorms.

"What on earth was that? And why now of all times?" said Lily as she settled on a coach in the small central living room of their new dorm "They would stand a better chance doing this when we had boarded? I mean then they would have the entire Moon Base to themselves, won't they?"

"Well, I think they have a different plan," said Sue "Having the Moon base would be an asset but the moment the next term comes it will be game over!"

"Right," said Lucy "But then, they are in contact with aliens. They could have exterminated the base entirely, am I right?"

"They seem to be quite dull..." began Lily, smirking "Or maybe on another level. There must be a reason for this! Definitely!"

"I think I've got it!" said Sam, suddenly giving everyone a spook "They can't give up so many opportunities at will, can they? They might have a bigger goal in mind. We can't be sure but I have a feeling."

"We'll just have to wait and see," said Lucy, cheerfully "Sue! We better get to work on that project!"

And the two of them hurried off.

"Well, I don't think their plan is a simple one," Lily sighs. "It feels like this is bigger than it seems."

"I think we have already seen them," said Sam suddenly. "The perpatrators."

"Well, how about we both track them down then?" suggested Lily "I am sure it's them. Sue will brush this off and Lucy won't think it's them from that one scene. I think we should tell Dr John wherever he is."

Lily searched for Dr John's number. She could swear he had given it to them. She found it a minute later and called him. Sam was looking hopefully - hoping that they could contact him.

"Yes," answered a voice on the phone which belonged to Dr John.

"Dr John! I think we are onto something!" Lily beamed.

"What is it?"

"Where are you? Can we meet you? I think we know who did it to the ship."

"Interesting... Meet me at the cafeteria at 6 tomorrow. "

"6?!" Lily exclaimed, devastated at the aspect of waking up early.

"In the evening,"

"Wait... Are all of you in on this?"

"Just me and Sam. I know this cannot be a coincidence. Believe me! We saw them."

"Anyway, I needed to divide the team into groups of two. Meet me there and I will tell you everything. I met with Dr Jones and Smith. They will also have a chat with us. Call Lucy and Sue when they do."

"Alright!"

"Oh yes and don't tell them about this just yet. There are some matters related to that."

"What?! Those two?!"

"I will explain there. Good night!"

"Good night!" said Lily, hanging up. "Sam, we have to meet up with Dr John - tomorrow at 6."

"Sure!" said Sam. "So, he believed you?"

"Yeah. I will tell you everything in the morning, I want to sleep!"

Sam and Lily both went to bed after that.

XX

The Meeting

The next day, they headed out at 6 after finishing work at 4 in the afternoon. It was late considering they usually get off work much earlier at 2 or 3 in the afternoon. That day, they had a building job - rebuilding the ship's landing pad - and due to technical difficulties (Sam forgetting to get his tool kit), they took longer to finish.

There were many people there now. Afterall, most people were done with their work by then. Sam and Lily were tired after that.

"Great! You are here," he greeted Lily and Sam "So, who did you exactly see?"

"Well, it was a researcher and a guard. The research I swear- Wait who did you put in-charge of the... you know?" asked Lily, immediately after sitting down.

"Frank, Frank Miller. One of the most trustworthy."

"I could have sworn he was with the guard. The guard had dragged him out with him. I think he was threatening him!" said Lily suddenly after a moment's silence.

"Are you sure?" asked Dr John, concerned.

"It was definitely him! The guard dragged him away after he tried to talk to us," said Sam.

There was pause.

"I will investigate this," said Dr John after a while "Frank was not there after the incident so…"

"Well, I think the guard was not a guard," said Sam "If he was, wouldn't we know him?"

"Yeah, I couldn't recognise him," said Lily "Believe me! I would know!"

"Noted," sighed Dr John "Anyway, I spoke with Dr Jones and Smith on what I had assigned to you and they want you to sign a form and join the guards.

"Oh yes! And Lucy, she was a student of Martina. From what I heard and what we knew of her students, cannot be trusted. She was one of her closest students.

"Even though she is not on her side now, she is a weak spot. Martina can exploit her so we have to somehow not involve her in the main plot while not letting Sue or her know about it."

"Wait? Are you serious?" exclaimed Lily, outraged, getting up from her chair"You seriously think it would be her of all people?!"

"Yeah! How can you just assume so?" Sam asked loudly as he too got up, "I am sure she won't be on her side! She can't be!"

"I know," sighed Dr John "I know but there is always the possibility. Dr Jones and Smith don't want to take any chances this time."

"So, then," said Lily, heavily "What's the plan?"

"We'll tell you. Go grab a snack and also call Lucy and Sue," said Dr John.

After that, Sam went to get Lucy and Sue while Lily went to get snacks.

When Sam got to the dorm, Sue and Lucy were working on what looked like a drone. Curious...

"What are you guys doin-?" asked Sam.

Both Sue and Lucy jumped, throwing a screw driver and file at him. Both of which, Sam dodged, catching the screw driver and file simultaneously. After that, he stared at them for an awkward moment.

"Umm, ok," said Sam, finally breaking the silence "Dr John called you guys."

"Wait wha-?" Sue stummered, "Wait really?"

"Yes..."

"Where are we supposed to go? asked Lucy.

"Follow me."

They followed Sam to the cafeteria, through the hallway between the cafeteria and the dorms. Sam tried to ask them what they were doing but they just lectured him on minding his own business and that it was a special project.

They got there a few minutes later. Lily and Dr John were deep in conversation.

"You sure you can do this?" Dr John asked "You two alone?"

"Of course! Don't underestimate us, we are much better than-," said Lily and glanced over to Sue and Lucy who were now right beside the table.

"We can surely do it!" she said quickly after that.

"Good! You two are here! Are you done with 'that'?" asked Dr John as he noticed them as well.

"Almost," said Sue, enthusiastically "Got the final touches left."

"Amazing!"

"Oh, sir! You are here!" said Dr John as he turned around and bowed down to Dr Jones and Smith. The others did the same.

"Good evening!" smirked Dr Jones "Come to our office. We'll tell you what you have to do."

They followed Dr Jones and Smith to their office without a word. They walked up a staircase to a wide room with the same two desks.

"You changed the location, right?" asked Sam as they entered "It was different before."

"Yeah, it got too crowded," said Dr Smith.

Dr Jones walked over to the projector lying on his desk, turned it on, spread a rolled up video foil on one of the windowed walls and pointed the projector towards it.

The image on the projector was of a mysterious script with no translation of any sort. Then Dr Smith spoke.

"This... is the reason why we are here. This is the script the People of Harrison spoke in. It was also found on a tomb in Greece. The occupant of the tomb however wasn't Greek.

"It looked like someone from the west but we can't be sure. The decorations of the tomb were also... strange. It depicted mysterious humanoid figures - which resembled the People of Harrison. The occupant also shared some features with the Harrisonians."

Dr Jones switched the image to a grotesque mummified corpse. It had long arms and longer fingers, its mouth covered, eyes closed.

Sam and Lily gagged. Sue and Lucy shrieked at the sight.

"All the artifacts and the occupant went missing just a year before we sued the cult and before the People of Harrison were discovered."

There was a long silence.

"We created the guard as protection against the cult. They are quite powerful and can have their way. We are not exactly at an advantage here," said Dr Jones, the atmosphere was now strangely tense and serious "You will have to spy on the cult. Are you sure you want to get involved in this? If not, you may remain silent until we erase your memories."

"We are sure!" exclaimed Sam and Lily at the same time.

"Us two!" exclaimed Sue and Lucy.

"Great, great! Amazing!" said Dr John, brightly.

"We'll update you tomorrow. Meet us at the cafeteria - eight in the morning. Good night!" said Dr Smith "Oh yeah and you're off work until a few days,"

"Great!" exclaimed Lily on their way back to their dorm.

The others also rejoiced as they would get a day off after quite some time.

XXI

The Security Unit

The next day, Sue woke everyone up early. She woke even before Lucy. Now, not only Sam and Lily were groggy but Lucy too. Sue however was now in a very pleasant mood. They skipped breakfast on Sue's insistance.

They trenched groggily their way to the cafeteria - everyone except Sue - a few minutes later, at 8: 35. Lily and Sue were in a heated debate on whether this was a sensible decision. And when they arrived, they were early and got some breakfast.

"Wow... Sue. You are really... um excited!" said Lucy with all the enthusiasm she could muster up, half asleep.

Sue made a proud speech and then they waited for the others.

Dr John came ten minutes later with a coffee. Dr Jones and Smith were fifteen minutes late.

"Well, then. Let's get to business," said Dr Smith "The Security Unit is a secret sector of SCI.CORP. It was created after the alien sighting as a precaution. The cult is quite powerful..."

"Manipulative..." Dr Jones muttered, darkly "They've slipped their way out of many things. It is really..." he cut off the sentence in a quiet whisper.

"Let's go somewhere more private," said Dr John.

They headed out of the cafeteria which was now filled with staff and through an unusually dark corridor. The corridor was messier than the rest of the base, having screws and other faults clearly visible unlike the other corridors.

It was quite long and there were no windows, only shaky looking doors on occasion. At the end of the corridor there was a heavy door like the ones near the exits except this one had a password lock. It looked like a high security prison.

Dr Jones stepped forward and typed in a password the door opened and they all stepped into a shabby cramped little room with a table and a few chairs.

They sat down.

"This is the headquarters of the Security Unit or Sector," said Dr Jones "This is where we meet up."

"Are there other people as well, like for say the guards?" asked Sue.

"Yes, of course. The guards are also part of the unit," said Dr John.

"Now then, we discovered that Frank Miller has been missing ever since the landing. I believe the cult is responsible," said Dr John "Your first task is to find him and bring him back without raising suspicion. We will give fake identities and all. You have to spy on the cult."

"If the cult was such a threat, why did you let them onto the ship?" asked Lily with suspicion.

"Yes we did," sighed Dr Smith "We thought that a fresh start was needed. It has been some time since they last interfered with our work and there is no use holding onto the past.

"So, we assigned them all to Team SSRS and let them live aboard the ship. If we hadn't, they'd not be here. But after the explosion and all that, we really didn't have a choice in the matter."

"We tolerated their 'mishaps' until the incident. It is not logical to do so."

"They will be sent to you and you will come later in the evening to put your disguises on," said Dr Jones, brightly "And remember the names until then!"

"Alright!" beamed Sue and Lucy. Sam and Lily nodded and they headed back.

As they walked through the corridor, staring curiously at the unappealing yet intriguing doors they passed. Many of them were covered in caution tape.

When they arrived at their dorm, they immediately checked their mail.

"I better get a good name!" said Sam and he checked.

"Yeah, yeah," sighed Lily "I really don't care as long as it is acceptable. I mean we finally got something new to do,"

"Amazing!" exclaimed Lucy "My name is Stella Jos,"

"Mine is Stella Johanson," said Sue "Really... um uncommon name,"

Sam let out a silent scream as he stared down on his name on Sue's laptop.

"Why did I get the name Frank?!" exclaimed Sam after a few moments.

"Surname?" asked Lily.

"Miller," sighed Sam.

"Wow..." sighed Lily.

After they memorized their names -which was not at all a problem for Sam, they headed back through the dark corridor later in the evening. The little was as cramped as before. There were wigs and name-tags scattered on a coffee table.

Dr John was waiting for them there.

"Have you remembered the names?" asked Dr John.

"Yes..." sighed Sam as he slouched down on a chair.

a"Good! I have your outfits and wigs. Oh, Sam! You have to wear a blond wig,"

Sam let out an exasperated silent scream.

"Why do I have to?! You already named me Frank Millar, are you trying to make me a copy? Is this not enough!" exclaimed Sam.

"Look, one Frank is missing, so we need another. Meh, I came up with it. Thought it would be unique."

"Don't you think it would be suspicious?"

"Nope. It is actually less obvious,"

"I just don't want to copy Frank. I mean, are you trying to make me a duplicate?"

"Don't worry you'll know soon enough."

Sam gives up on his debate and they put on their costumes.

Sue enthusiastically put on her name-tag and round glasses. Sam reluctantly put on his costume which was a wig and a name-tag. Lily also got a wig - a blond one - and had to dress very neatly. Lucy stayed the same.

"Now, you each will meet with Dr Jones and get to know your role," said Dr John "Sam you are first! You know what Lily, you go too. It will be helpful later."

Dr John led the two of them out and through the corridor. They went through a door close by. It was pretty clean but not locked too tightly.

Dr John pushed the door open and Dr Jones was sitting behind a table. They headed in and Sam and Lily sat down on the other side.

"You both came?" said Dr Jones as Dr John prepared to leave.

"Oh, I thought it'd be helpful," said Dr John as he closed the door behind himself.

"Oh... Anyway, Sam, you have to act as a decoy for us to rescue Frank. First, you need to join the cult and then once you are close enough to them try to get to Frank and do... something and get him out," said Dr Jones.

"So, I have got to figure out that 'something' out on my own?" said Sam after a few moments.

"Yeah, I think you can. Anyway, Lily will work with you so, you both can work together,"

"Fine..." sighed Sam

"And Lily, you are also going into the cult. You will help Sam and you both will keep ties. Also, Lucy will go into the cult. Keep an eye on her. If she gets in with them-"

"She won't!" exclaimed Lily.

"Can you at least trust her?!" Sam exclaimed as well.

"Alright... Just make sure she does her work."

"Fine..." sighed Lily.

"Your new team is Team RSTR. Remember. And call the other two in. Might as well do it in pairs,"

Sam and Lily called Sue and Lucy and took them to the same room. They were there for half an hour and Sue looked particularly cross when they finally exited the room. She kept muttering to herself.

Lucy looked nervous. Sam and Lily guessed that Dr Jones had told Sue about Lucy.

They got back to their dorm and the first thing Sam did was throwing his wig onto the couch and getting on his phone. Lily went to her room.

In all, they just lounged for the rest of the day.

XXII

Into the Cult We Go

The next day (their second day off work), they got a message from Dr John.

Sue was the first to get the message and let everyone read it from her laptop. The message said the following:

Dear Team RSTR (SSTR),

You will be starting on your task from today. Also remember, do not under any circumstance break disguise. If you have an issue, inform us!

Don't send the information on the usual email. Send it on rstr.team@sci.corp.org. Stay safe!

Regards

Dr John.

The Message

"Wait, we are starting today?!" said Sam, shocked. "I thought I wouldn't have to wear that wig for a week!"

"Oh, come on. It's not that bad," said Lily "I have to wear one too, you know,"

"We better search for the cult," said Sue, enthusiastically w"It is going to be a ride,"

They head out. It was still early and they had some time.

After searching for a while, they came across a woman wearing strange clothes; a maroon hoodie with a weird symbol on the back of it, ripped jeans and large round sunglasses.

Lucy hurried over to her to talk to her

Sam stared at her, confused.

After a while she returned with the woman.

"Heard you were looking for us," the woman beamed "Myself Selina, from the good place. Come with me!"

The others stared at Lucy. The 'good place' what did she mean?

Selina acted as though she knew them well and was in a lively conversation with Lucy, using many terms like 'the good place' in it.

"What did you do?" Sue muttered to her as their conversation drew to a close.

"Don't worry. She'll trust us now," said Lucy, smirking cheekily.

Selina led them to a laboratory that looked abandoned and then down a trap door leading to a secret underground passage. It was dark, only lit by a few LEDs. The passage was long - by Lily's estimates it led to a place far away from the base, most probably underground.

Sue suspected that this was where that cult was hiding out.

They arrived at an underground chamber which was much like the base a few minutes later. It was surprisingly big, almost as big as the base. The chamber was decorated with many sheets of maroon cloth and the cult's symbol. Hooded individuals seemingly blended in with the environment.

Selina looked on proudly.

"Pretty good place!" she said suddenly. "Come on, how can we see everything in one day?"

Then she practically led them through the whole chamber. After a she arrived at a dark room, beaming. At this point, they began to really appreciate the sheer size of the chamber. It was almost as big as the base and looked like it had been built recently.

"And here's our best helper!" she beamed, pointing at someone familiar. "We keep a watch on him!"

There was a familiar person sitting tied up in a chair inside the dark room.

It was Frank! Lily recognised him at once.

"So, I was right," she muttered to herself, half shocked, half happy that she was right. "What is the cult planning on doing now?"

XXIII

Escape Plan

They stared for a moment.

Frank did not take notice.

They asked Selina if there was a room they could stay in as they were now tired. Selina led them to a spacious room with four beds and left.

Almost immediately after she left, Sue began her cleanliness check.

"Are you sure this is necessary?" groaned Lily.

"So, our health is less necessary?" argued Sue.

After a heated debate and half an hour, she was certain the room was clean.

Then they sat down to talk.

"That was definitely him!" said Lily.

"But why is he still here?" asked Sam "I mean, the cult got out and all."

"They might have a plan," said Lucy "I heard some hooded people talking near us.

"They said something like this in the cult's language 'We can use a hostage' said one, 'Too obvious, let's just use him for information,' said another. That's all I heard."

"Hmm..." sighed Lily "I have a plan! Sam, you will go and break him out then replace him until we can get him out of here. And then, you can sneak out on your own. How's the plan?"

"You are staying with me," said Sam "We can use the cloaks they wear to sneak out and I need to get my hands on one somehow,"

"Fine..."

"Good plan!" said Lucy, happily "I'll be leaving tomorrow to Dr John's place for some work. Sad, I can't join you," she sighed.

"There are plenty of other things!" said Sue, "This is nothing! We have a lot more fun stuff to do later. Don't worry!"

And one motivational speech later, Sam, Lily and Lucy went out to get cloaks. They luckily bumped into Selina on their way to the cloak stand she had shown them.

"Heya!" she called out to them.

"Hello! Good to see you. We were just looking for cloaks if we can get them," said Sam.

"Of course you can. Four, right? I'll get them for you!"

"Actually, five. Lily here is clumsy," said Sam, as Lily glared at him.

They got the cloaks and headed back.

The next day, Sam, Lily and Sue went to the room where Frank was early in the morning, wearing their cloaks. Lily and Sue got him untied and Sue and Frank hurried off. Sam replaced Frank in his position and Lily stayed there with the extra cloak under hers.

After a while, some people came into the room. Once everyone had left, Sam slipped the cloak on and the both hurried out.

When they reached the passage, they met Sue and Frank and hurried back through the passage and through the trap door. Then they dropped Frank off at an infirmary.

By the time they made it back to their dorm and had changed, it was early noon and Lucy was there waiting for them.

"So," she said, hopefully "Did it work?"

"Yes!" sighed Sam, slumping down on the couch in the centre of the dorm and grabbing his phone.

They went to meet with Dr John in the evening to tell him what they had seen. Dr John was waiting for them in the same place where Dr Jones explained their disguises. They finished explaining in an hour.

"Really..." said Dr John, after a while "Those cloaks you've got. We can do something. Oh yeah, call Frank. He's in for a ride."

He went to get Frank.

"What's the plan?" asked Sam, curiously.

"Sam, remember Frank Miller?"

"Don't talk about it! I had to stay up there!" exclaimed Sam.

"Don't worry," reassured Dr John "I only want Frank to tell us what all he saw during his time there. Simple. Oh yes and you are going back to work tomorrow."

Lucy was overjoyed meanwhile Sam and Lily let out an exasperated sigh.

Sue came back with Frank who looked utterly confused and rightly so. He glanced from one person to another in the room then greeted Dr John. They both sat down and then Dr John spoke.

"So, Frank Miller number 1, sorry Frank Miller, what did you get to know from your stay?"

Frank looked puzzled for a moment then spoke.

"What do you mean?" he asked.

"You know the people who you went with right?" asked Dr John.

"Yes..." he stammered.

"They are the Cult of Harrison, basically not trustworthy people."

"The cult of wha-"

"Harrison"

"Ok and I have to know about that?"

"Yes, they were the people who locked you up. I will explain later but can you tell us what all you heard?" aske Dr John, now slightly annoyed.

"Alright..." sighed Frank "They keep babbling on about some big takeover or something, no idea."

"Takeover," Sam repeated blankly.

"Yeah, I have no idea too," said Lucy.

"This could mean literally anything," said Lily, after a while.

"Correct," agreed Dr John "But I think I can guess what they mean. You explain to Frank what everything about the cult is but not that part and I'll be on my way,"

Dr John ushered them out

As they made their way out, Frank looked at them confused and utterly puzzled at what he had just heard as he followed them out.

"What the heck was that about?" he asked them.

"We'll tell you," said Lily "Come to our dorm."

"Ok," Frank said with a questioning look.

Once they got to their dorm, they told Frank everything about the cult.

"Okay, so you're saying that this cult is evil or something and you want to kick them out because of that. Is the cult also dangerous?" Frank summarized what he understood.

"Yeah basically that," said Lily.

"So, this was going on the entire time we were on the ship and all," asked Frank.

"Yes,"

After a while of talking, Frank left for work. And they went to bed early on Sue's command.

XXIV
Back To Work

The next day, everyone woke up considerably late and were tired - except Sue and a slightly less tired Lucy. Sam and Lily were half dead until breakfast.

"What did I tell you about waking up early everyday?" said Sue as finished packing up her things.

"Well, I really don't have an excuse this time," Lily muttered as they headed out.

That day, they had a small project and three tasks. Their tasks log was not packed. As they walked through the observatory which they had seen for the first time, they really began to appreciate the progress the teams had made.

There were greenhouses with transparent windows and special pumps that extract oxygen from water on the left. Then on the right, there were solar panels connected to a station to convert the light energy into electricity.

There were many new structures and it seemed a terraform mission was going to be under way soon.

"So, we have to create a file sorting AI that can sort files on command for the project," Sue began to recite in a monotonous tone as they sat down in the cafeteria. "Then we have to fix one of the solar panels - I have never seen the ones they have here up close before - great! Then we have to supervise a research team - our first supervision! Then to top it off, we have to check if Greenhouse 05 is in order,"

"We've never been to any of the greenhouses before. I believe they are new!" said Lucy as they went to the IT Department for their first project.

They got to work. By noon, they were done with most of the code and went to the cafeteria to eat.

"You know, it's crazy to think that only years ago, these tasks would have taken months," said Lily as she drank coffee "And that's all thanks to the new kinetic energy power-plants that started popping up."

"Well, that's all new," said Sue, who took the longest to finish her part. "I prefer the traditional way. No mishaps. Part of being responsible!"

Lucy then complimented and chatted with Sue about work.

"The project's due tomorrow, right?" asked Sam as they walked over towards the right of the base for their first task.

"Yeah," said Lily, who was browsing her tablet.

They walked up to one of the exits which had the usual warning sign and through the door.

The outside was spectacular. The structures construction projects looked much bigger from the outside. Team SSTR gazed around them in awe. Even through the slightly tinted lens of the space suit, it looked amazing.

In minutes, they went to work on fixing the solar panel. All their work went smoothly that day and all the days following it.

In the months after, the base got drastically bigger and there were many more new things. An observatory to gaze at stars. Many more solar panels and someone had invented a new tool that made it easier to cut metals like steel.

And so, the desolate planet of Mars was transformed into a lively place resembling Earth. Many new and ambitious projects were being executed.

XXV
Mission Enceladus

It was yet again a normal day for Team SSTR. Their life had almost returned to how it was before on Earth. They had now mostly forgotten about the cult - with occasional side missions as a small reminder. Today was that sort of day.

Team SSTR strolled down the same corridor and its doors now, familiar with it.

They entered a clean door and sat down. Dr John, Dr Jones and Dr Smith were waiting for them.

"Hello!" greeted Dr John "We have come to an agreement. The cult will remain docile if we allow them to do their thing away from the base."

"What?!" exclaimed Lily "Do you really think that would be safe?!

"Well, we have our precautions. Please continue work as usual. We won't be facing any more problems!"

"Okay... So, we are supposed to?" asked Sam.

"Just act normal and stay alert. You will make weekly visits to the cult just in case," explained Dr John.

"Alright..." they sighed.

"Your visit is tomorrow!" Dr Smith called after them.

And so, Team SSTR went the following day to the cult. They were told to just check in with them.

"I don't know why they trust people so much," sighed Lily as they walked through the underground passage.

"Lily, they have their reasons," said Sue.

"Welp, we just have to walk through and ask some folks right?" said Sam, hoping it won't take too long. "We even got to work today!"

"You are lazy," said Sue.

"Whatever!"

They finished their check-up quickly - suspiciously quickly. No one at the hideout seemed to mind their company. Strangely, as they checked everything in their normal attire, the cult's members didn't retaliate as they did before.

The next day, they were assigned to a new project to establish a colony on Saturn's moon, Enceladus. They had mixed feelings to say the least.

"This is a great opportunity to expand our knowledge and promote our status," said Sue, excitedly. "No one's ever started a project besides ours."

"I know, but with the cult around?" questioned Lily.

"You are speculating!" disagreed Sue.

"There is a chance...," suggested Sam.

"Conspiracy theorists!" exclaimed Sue "Been like this from the start! Find something to complain about anywhere!"

"Come on!" moaned Lily.

Lucy meanwhile had left the three to debate on the matter minutes ago. A few minutes later, the argument ended and they went to bed.

The next day, Team SSTR was called to a meeting to introduce them to the other teams assigned to the mission and to discuss the progress they were making. They had to go to LAB-308 which was close to their dorm, being only a floor below the dormitories.

When they arrived at the meeting, they found a cheery and happy atmosphere. Everyone was energetic and eager.

They quickly settled down and the in-charge of the mission spoke.

"We have made significant progress, and we will plan a mission to the Moon very soon. Now, it's Phase 4 of the plan when we start sending people and satellites. Work will begin tomorrow and welcome to the team!

"You will receive an email on all the timings tomorrow. Also, myself, Dr Dale. Team SSER will meet you at the cafeteria beside the Chinese food stall. They will explain everything.

"That's all! Meeting's over!"

"Well, looks like we're late for the action," said Lily as they headed back.

"Still! We are moving fast!" said Lucy excitedly.

"All the troubles in the world are gone and we can relax!" sighed Sam.

"Don't forget the cult still exists," said Lily, slyly.

"You really do have an affinity for conspiracy theories!" said Sue. "It's a good day. Don't bring that into it."

"Fine..."

The next day, they went to meet up with Team SSER.

XXVI
Mission Gone Wrong

"Wonder how they're going to be," said Lucy, excitedly.

"Ehh, doesn't matter," shrugged Lily.

When they got there, Team SSER was waiting for them.

"Heya!" greeted a blond, cheery looking man.

"Hello," said Sam, sitting down beside him.

The others sat down.

"I am Brianna. Greetings," said a dull woman sitting opposite to them in a tired tone.

"Greetings, Brianna. I am Lily," said Lily in the same tone.

"Nice to meet you," said Brianna.

"Hello! I am Selina," said an energetic looking woman sitting beside Lucy.

Lucy introduced herself and they both started talking about the mission.

"Alright, it's just us three. One of our members defected," said Brianna dully.

"So, found a new one yet," asked Lily as she sat beside her.

"Nah,"

"How was the 'defector'?"

"Not bad. Could be better,"

After chatting for a while, Team SSER explained the mission.

"So, you're kind of late in joining the mission," began Brianna in a monotonous tone. "We're going to start work on sending satellites to Enceladus. Work on Phase 4** will officially start tomorrow but today you all can go over the plans. I will send it and you can do the assigned work,"

** The phase when the spacecraft and satellites are prepared for lift off.

Team SSTR then got to work on learning the plans.

"Do we have any work today?" asked Lily as she finished learning the plans.

"Yes," said Sue, excitedly.

Over the following days, the mission had Sue, Sam, Lily and Lucy too preoccupied to think more about their weekly trips to the hide-out; even overlooking minor suspicious activity.

Once, the cult members were speaking in their secret language - a violation of one of the terms of the agreement and Sam just let it slide with a small punishment. Sue on the other hand over-criticised everything.

One time, she mistook a card for a secret document - that didn't end well.

While their weekly trips were lousy, their work on the project was impressive and the first satellite was due to launch in a week - 2 weeks before the deadline.

"This is one of the best projects we've worked on!" said Sue as they headed back to their dorm after work.

"I just hope nothing happens on the day of the launch, we have been shortlisted," began Sam "If we get there, we can finally do a Moon mission that didn't involve a resource shortage or anything like that,"

"Be positive!" exclaimed Lucy "If you think that way, something will happen!"

"But-" began Lily.

"No buts!" exclaimed Lucy.

"Fine," sighed Sam.

The next day, Team SSTR was bombarded with tasks. While working on the mission, they had progressively been getting more and more important roles. Now, they were in the top five or so crucial teams.

This had its benefits but the workload was, let's just say, not the best part. They even skipped visits to the hide-out.

"So," Sue recited first thing after breakfast "We have to recheck the supplies, estimate if we might need extra resources, test the reinforced material the ship is made off, edit the spacesuits and lastly record all the information!"

"Wow, we got less work today," said Lucy as they headed out.

"Less?!" exclaimed Lily as they went through the lift and onto the second floor where they worked "It's more than what we got yesterday!"

"Oh, come on," sighed Sue. "Me and Lucy always do extra work on top of what we get and we still have the stamina to work on our own projects. You were saying?"

"Wow," said Sam. "Not really a fan of over-working but I could give it a try,"

"Good luck!" chuckled Lily as she walked past him. "You can try for a week."

"Nope!"

And so another eventful day went by.

A few days later, it was almost the day of the launch. A sudden development. Even Sue was caught off guard.

Then, almost suddenly, it was the day of the launch. Everyone was tense because when they set off for Earth's Moon, they at least had done it before but this was new.

Team SSTR and some other teams including Team SSER would be going to Enceladus.

After changing into their spacesuits, they were chatting.

"Welp, this is our third time being blasted out into space," said Lily "How 'bout you all?"

"Second," signed Brianna "Not a fan really."

"Same, you go through so much only to have the most stressful time of your life ,"

"I know!"

"Could you at least appreciate that we are a part of the mission?!" exclaimed Sue.

"A bit. Our ranks increased and all," said Lily.

"That's all I can expect I guess," sighed Sue.

"It's almost time!" Daniel said as he rushed to call them to check their suits for a second time. "Just gotta check our suits again,"

"Alright!" said Selina as she hurried off to a changing room.

A few minutes later, everything was prepared for the launch. Huge solar-powered rockets stood on stands ready to take off. Team SSTR was now checking the statistics.

And then, when they had least expected it...

Bang!

The largest rocket which had once stood firm on its stand blew up. Then proceeding that, the other two rockets at its side blew up. The sound was deafening.

Massive rockets were reduced to smithereens. All of the researchers and crew working on the mission - who were camping a temporary site near the launch site - rushed for the exits to the passage leading back to the main base.

They had not anticipated such an incident - at all. Not knowing what to do, the in-charge, Dr Dale rushed everyone out of the site. Nobody had really considered the bizarreness of the incident in the light of shards of matter being flung in all directions.

The windows were now shattered and the site a mess. Everyone either went through the passage that connected it to the base or out in spacesuits. Team SSTR went out in their spacesuits which they were already wearing. They and the others ran around looking for the nearest exit.

The run there seemed to take forever and was discoordinated and in the fray, they got lost...

Panic soon arose as they couldn't find their way back. They could survive in the suits for only so long.

"What are we going to do now?!" complained Lily "We just got blasted and now this!"

"Wait, there is a map on the suit's arm," said Sam "Check where we are!"

"We're not far from... a strange block," said Lily after checking.

"Block?" asked Lucy as she too checked the map. "Yes, there is an unlabelled block,"

"Well, let's check it out," said Sam. "Unreported buildings, I am pretty sure aren't allowed."

"Ok..." Sue agreed reluctantly. "But, don't you think we should report this to Dr John or someone first?"

"It won't take long!" said Lily.

"Come on, we could do with some time outside," added Lucy.

"Fine..."

XXVII

The Secret Elevator

And so they headed towards the block. Upon closer inspection, it seemed to be an elevator. It was shabby and looked old. The buttons still worked but not well - they kept blinking an ominous green. The elevator itself was a dark grey.

Sam mistrustfully pressed the only button which had an arrow pointing down. The elevator doors opened instantly and waited for them to enter. Cautiously, they entered.

Where the elevator went? They didn't know. Why was it there? They didn't know.

But, for all they knew - they couldn't tell how - it had something to do with what had just happened.

The elevated reopened to a dark hexagonal room. It was laced with velvet of a dark maroon. The cult's symbol plastered on the velvet. The floor had a velvet carpet of the same maroon. There was what looked to be a hexagonal roof above them. There was a strange device on the carpet surrounded by an elaborately drawn yellow chalk circle. It was big enough for 12 people to sit 3 feet away from each other.

The first layer consists of 12 hexagons each big enough for a person to sit in them. The second layer was an indecipherable text written, looking as though it was upside-down. The third layer was an intricate pattern of hexagons all with one point pointing towards the centre. The fourth and final layer was simple, only a thin circle surrounding the device.

The device was a hexagonal prism with many inscriptions. It had what looked to be a mini projector in its centre and buttons on each corner. It too was maroon. Its buttons and projector, golden.

What was it?

The friends hesitated. This could be a trap.

"What is this place?" muttered Lily in a mix of awe and suspicion.

"No idea," said Sam.

"What's that?" asked Sue, pointing at the strange device.

"Looks like a project" said Lily who went an inch closer to examine it.

"What for?" asked Sam.

"Don't know," said Lucy "I have never seen this!"

"Pretty big," gasped Sam, looking around "Let's take a look!"

"Sure!" beamed Lily "It will be something exciting at last,"

"Hey!" snapped Sue "Shh! Quiet! Someone might be watching, Shouldn't we report this first?"

"Nah!" replied Sam.

Sue sighs. "Let's explore."

So, they wander around the sizable room. It was bigger than it looked at first glance. There was a hallway leading inside what seemed to be another room.

They went into the hallway which was to plastered with the strange symbols. This hallway was different from the ones they saw in the hideout. There were doors lining its parallel walls. Why would this be here?

These were like the symbols on Martina's cloak when they had seen it. As they walked through, there was a meeting room at the end.

"What's going on?" asked Sam as he heard voices from inside the room. "Shh... something interesting's going on,"

They ducked behind a door nearby and listened intently but to no avail.

Inside the room, two hooded people were talking. They were speaking in the secret language. They were whispering. They were saying somethings in English like base, but they were random. The two spoke for five minutes then left.

"What was that all about?" asked Sam as they prepared to leave after they watched the two people hurry by.

"Don't know," said Lily as she opened the door to see if the coast was clear then got out.

"We better get out of here!" hissed Sue "Our suits are almost out of power and someone might hear us,"

"Good idea!" Lucy agreed.

"But no one can hear us, we are talking through our suits," said Lily as they all headed back.

"That's not the point!" Sue hissed again "With our bulky suits anyone can spot us!"

"Fine," sulked Lily.

The team headed back quickly but when they got to the room, eleven cult members were sitting in the drawn hexagons, holding their hands together while crossing fingers. There were twelve others standing behind them doing the same.

They were chanting something in the strange language.

The team ducked in a door in the hallway just in to avoid one more cult member rushing in to complete the circle. Then, the roof which was divided in half they noticed now as they peeped through the door, split into two to reveal a smaller clear glass window.

The projector turned on, sending a bright beam of light up through the window and the whole room lit up.

The team stared on in awe. What is going on?

"We need to get out of here!" hissed Sue.

"Yeah," agreed Lily "It's creepy..."

"But how?" asked Sam.

"We'll just have to wait and pray that no one finds us," sighed Lily "But seriously what is this place?"

"Don't know," whispered Lucy, looking shocked.

"I have a plan!" said Lily "We make a run for it one by one. That way it will be less conspicuous. There will also be a slimmer chance we are caught,"

"But," argued Sue, "Only one of us by ourselves won't be safe either. If something happens and the one gets caught there won't be a chance of escape. They have more than ten people here and we are four,"

"Point..." sighed Lily. "Let's see..."

Meanwhile outside, the cult members had finished chanting and were dispersing. Ceasing the opportunity, the team escaped all at once through the elevator.

"Why did we not follow the plan?" complained Sue as they ran to the base.

"Well, it was in person, much creepier so..." said Lily.

"Definitely!" exclaimed Lucy. "There were spiders!"

"So?"

"Anyways, let's get back to base," said Sam.

XXVIII

Back To Base

They arrived at the main base that looked different from before. The windows were tinted and doors locked. They rushed to the nearest entrance to find it guarded.

The guard let them into a small cramped space and told them to take off their suits and change into a shirt and pants. He ushered them into a changing room.

"Who are y'all?" asked the guard after they had changed.

"Team SSTR," answered Lily.

"Team SSTR eh, we've been looking for you all. Wait where have you been?"

"Got lost" replied Lily.

"Your names,"

"Lily Carter," said Lily.

"Samuel Johnson," said Sam.

"Sue Susan," said Sue.

"Lucy Abott,"

"Checks out, please go through the face scan,"

The team each got their face scanned against their registered photos and then registered new photos and were let in.

"What's with all the security measures," complained Lily "What happened?"

"Well," sighed Sue "There was a full-fledged attack on the base an hour ago, wonder why,"

"Not that," said Lily "But what is actually going on? Who attacked us? Why was there an underground block somewhere on Mars?!"

"Well," sighed Sue again "It is because of all that!"

"But this should have taken longer to do right?" argued Sam "All this security procedure stuff needs at least a year to build!"

"Yes, strange..." mumbled Lily, speeding up from walk to a run "Wait, I have a theory. Quick! To Dr John!"

"What?!" exclaimed Sue "Now?! We just got here!"

"It's important!" hissed Lily as she ran ahead while the others struggled to keep up. They rushed along the halls fast.

Sue kept up with Lily while questioning what had gotten into her. Sam and Lucy stumbled behind unsure what to do. It was strange that all this security protocol was there in less than a day.

Was this some sort of precaution? It seemed strange... Why was all this happening? What was going on?

As they all asked themselves to no avail, they had reached the corridor. A guard was walking out with a serious expression on his face.

"Where is Dr John?" asked Lily, impatiently.

"Second room ahead from here," he answered, dumbfounded.

"Thanks," said Lily as she and the others rushed off.

Lily barged into the room where Dr John was sitting, looking over papers, jumping when he saw her and the others.

"What in the world?!" he exclaimed "Where were you all?"

"Long story," gasped Sam, out of breath as he and Lucy let themselves in after Lily and Sue.

"Okay..."

Lily looked dead serious and Sue looked frustrated meanwhile Sam and Lucy gazed around the room, lost. Lily sat herself down. Sue did the same along with Sam and Lucy too.

"Did you know?" began Lily with a strong hint of sarcasm "That there is a block somewhere out here,"

"A what?" stummered Dr John, confused.

"Yes, a block," confirmed Lily "Well, actually it's an elevator that looks like it's on its last leg. It leads to a creepy underground place that has a projector, perhaps in the center of an intricate circle for some reason. Make of it what you will,"

There was a long moment of silence. Even Sue needed to process everything that had happened in the last few hours. It felt like all of it was crammed into a single day.

"An elevator in the middle of nowhere," muttered Dr John. "You will have to show me that place. But before that, let me fill you in. The cult was responsible for the attack earlier today and is being investigated.

"You must've had a hard time getting in here, right?"

"Yeah! Security measures apparently," ranted Lily.

"Security measures get at least one day before all personnel can follow said measures," said Sam "Were all the guards trained to do this?"

"That..."

"Yes, I assume," said Lily.

"Correct... I had enforced this security measure,"

"So, your reasoning behind this was that you suspected something like this all along," questioned Sue, with skepticism.

"Not quite, there was something wrong, definitely. The cult hasn't been this docile in ages. The change in their attitude was too sudden. So, naturally we guessed we put in some minor precautions,"

"I don't believe training personnel and setting up the security methods etc is really minor," said Lucy "Practically, I would agree while the stakes are unlikely,"

"Yes! That's the whole point. It takes months for human brains to memorise a single concept at times!" said Lily, exasperated.

"Well, correct... again,"

"So then, I can assume you at least had a guess that something like this would happen?" asked Lily.

"Yes. It was just a prediction," sighed Dr John.

"So, what do we do now?!" asked Sam "I mean all this happened already, so what now?"

"We'll see, go back to the dorms,"

They spent the rest of the day thinking and arguing about what had happened.

XXIX

What WILL Happen Next?!

The next day, they woke up with a bang, literally. At around 6 in the morning, BANG! Smetherines went flying through the window in their dorm. Confused and bewildered, they hurried out in pajamas to check what had happened.

"What is it now!" exclaimed Lily, sounding clearly frustrated. "First one bombing then another! What the heck!"

"What do you expect?!" exclaimed Sue "They'd bomb us once and run off?!"

"Wow, so hilarious!" sighed Lily sarcastically as she plopped down on a chair and rocked back and forth on it.

There was a brief silence before someone rushed into the dorm.

"Um... Guys-" she began, timidly.

"What now!?" exclaimed Lily, her temper rising.

She walked over to the younger girl and asked her impatiently "What in the world is going on now?"

"Um... yes, um, the cult has attack... again," she said, nervously "Dr Jones and Smith are calling,"

"Thanks for the info," said Lily, having calmed down.

She then headed back to dress. So did Sam who had been drinking his coffee the whole time.

"Aren't you at least gonna call her in?" asked Sue.

No one heard.

Sue sighed heavily, thinking "What is it with them and being a responsible citizen?".

"Get in and sit down while we get ready," she said, ushering her in.

The girl walked in and sat down nervously on a chair. Then Sue went to change while Lucy, who had already dressed, made coffee.

They ran back, following the girl to Dr Jones and Smith. Hurriedly dressed and untidy.

When they arrived, the girl knocked on the door and said it was "Sally" before Dr Jones and Smith let them in. They sat down on the sofa in front of Dr Jones and Smith's desk.

After they had settled down, Dr Smith spoke.

"This is serious. We need to act. But first, let us fill you in-"

"Dr John already did," said Sam, interrupting.

"Oh... alright," sighed Dr Smith, disgruntled "So, we need to do something about the war situation. Let's cut the chase, we are launching an offensive."

"Wait, what?!" exclaimed Sue "Offensive. Has it really gotten that bad? Have you lost all communication with the cult?"

"Sadly, yes," said Dr Jones. "As we have no way to reason with them, we'll have to resort to the last possible option... Attack..."

The team all sat there frozen, shocked. Are just about to fight a war... ON MARS?! Relations with the cult were still peaceful until now, what happened?

Strange...

"You are sure, you know, this is right?" asked Lucy, nervously, looking like the girl from before who had left minutes ago.

"Yes," replied Dr Smith, harshly. "We have decided on this after much debate."

Lucy looked away, shunned. Sue glared at Dr Jones and Dr Smith. Sam and Lily looked away angrily.

"Well..." sighed Dr Smith, impatiently "If you were wondering, we did try to communicate, in many ways. So now, we have had on our ships from the start a Defence Department which was dedicated to the production of weapons.

"This was a project recommended by the government and we thought that it would be useful for landscaping here on Mars. And now we can test some of our weapons."

"What do you mean?" asked Sam with suspicion.

"Well," smirked Dr Jones "We'll have to show you."

He and Dr Smith got up and ushered them out of the room and led them further down the corridor. Much further, than they had ever gone before.

They then turned to the left following Dr Jones and Dr Smith. There was a metal wall. The team stared at it, confused.

Dr Jones said "Defence Department S 01,"

The metal broke into two and made way for them to enter, closing behind them as they did.

"Now," said Dr Smith, importantly "Don't tell anyone about this. Only a few know about it. We are telling you because we... need some of you to play a role in this mission,"

He briefly glanced and Lucy then continued "This is a confidential mission. Under any circumstance don't disclose the existence of this."

He then said "S 01," and a face recognition sensor appeared from the wall. Dr Jones asked each of them to come over after he typed something into the keyboard below the sensor.

They each stepped forward and then Dr Jones and Smith did.

Moments after that, the sensor and keyboard disappeared into the wall and the wall opened as though it was a door. They stepped in, in turns as the door was narrow and heard the door close behind them.

In front of them was a huge room. It was filled with a variety of guns, ammunition and other things. They were surprised to say the least. They didn't think all these military units would be required on a space colonisation mission. And yet they were all there.

Everything from nuclear weapons to rocket launchers.

"Some of this stuff is not necessary yet," said Dr Jones.

"What do you mean 'yet'?" asked Sue. "Do you really think you can't at least try and communicate?"

"Well-," sighed Dr Jones.

"Could we at least make sure that we are doing the right thing?" said Lucy.

Dr Jones and Smith both glared. "We will do as we see appropriate. Lily, Sam, and Sue come with us." said Dr Smith, ushering Lucy to the side.

Sue and the others followed them, disgruntled.

"Tomorrow exactly at 6 PM, we will launch our first attack." explained Dr Jones. "You will be there to help us manage the operation.

"Come to this room tomorrow."

"That's all," said Dr Smith "You can look around. We'll be starting a landscaping project later on after recycling all useful parts. There we'll be testing some of these; so take a good look,"

The team walked around. Sue wasn't quite in the best mood as she sulked. To which, Dr Jones and Dr Smith weren't pleased.

Lily, however, was fascinated and looked around attentively while discussing different things they could do with the machines with Sam. Lucy sulked with Sue.

They left later in the day with almost nothing to do. Lily had some things to code. Sue sorted some files and Sam worked on a broken model. Lucy hasn't spoken at all since then.

It was an uneventful day after seeing the weapons.

XXX

Attack!

The next day, they got a call from Dr John. It was 9 AM and they had all gathered to have breakfast. Sam and Lily, half awake, Sue, over-energetic and Lucy silent.

"Hello," answered Sam.

"Yes… yes. I'm sure you have heard of the plan on launching an offensive right?"

"Yes," Sam put the call on speaker. They all gathered to listen.

"Meet me at the cafeteria,"

He hung up.

"First, the bombings one and two, then, suddenly we learn that there is a whole military weapons storage here, then Dr John decides to call us for something," said Lily as she banged her coffee on the table "What is going on?! Why is all this happening now?! I remember the good old days when we had a STRESS FREE LIFE,"

"Yeah!" said Sam "We could do whatever!"

"Irresponsible," muttered Sue "Can you take note that the situation is dire?"

"Yeah," sighed Sam "Having seen through two bombings,"

"Why is everyone so vague?!" exclaimed Lily as she finished her coffee "Dr Jones and Smith didn't elaborate why exactly they had lost hope in the cult. When they showed us the weapons room or S 01, there were many more weapons than necessary for landscaping."

"Yeah," recalled Sam "Many of them looked like real last resort military weapons."

They both turned to Sue who looked very confused as she hadn't looked closely at the weapons. She shrugged.

"They are there for a reason, obviously," said Sue.

Sam shrugged "Not like they'd tell us,"

"Yeah," said Lily. "Let's relax for now,"

Beep! Beep! The phone rang again.

"Yes," answered Sam yet again.

"Come at 10 AM today," said Dr John hurriedly before hanging up again.

"Oh crap!" said Lily "We're running late. It's nine fifty five."

They hadn't changed from their pajamas yet.

"Hurry up and get ready!" commanded Sue.

Five minutes later, they were hurrying to the cafeteria.

There, Dr John was waiting for them at a table. He looked serious. They sat down quietly.

"So, they are launching an attack today," said Dr John, very quickly "It doesn't make sense. Before yesterday, Dr Jones and Smith were against the idea of war, proposed by some. Then they got a message or something and completely changed their attitude."

"Right," said Lily, trying to process what Dr John had said.

"So, what are we going to do?" asked Sam.

"Don't know," said Dr John.

Lucy did not speak. She hadn't the whole time.

"Um, how about exploring the block from earlier," she said, sounding like someone with a cold.

They all went quiet then stared at her for a few moments.

"Actually," said Sue after a while. "That's a good idea!"

The others agreed.

Later in the day, Dr John had gotten them permission to get out and explore. They were outside and heading straight for the block.

"Why are they setting up a secret base?" said Sam as they reached the elevator and Dr John began to examine it.

"Don't know," replied Dr John, distractedly almost in a trance more to himself than Sam. "In fact, there hasn't been a single row since we put the cult under control... Strange. Seven security checks and nothing suspicious...

The team listened attentively and quietly, hoping to get a clue.

"I would have figured they had realised the error of their way. Not so, probably. My knowledge on the subject is so limited it's embarrassing! I should've paid more attention to it when it came up in my time. Well, I can't guess or predict their intentions because my exposure to the cult is limited..."

He sighed heavily and then said "We should check this out. I'll have to see for myself. I do apologise for my lack of knowledge on the subject but either way it would be better to check it out."

"Right!" the team responded.

They were now going down the elevator once again. Only this time, Dr John was examining every last inch of it. When he was done, he repeated the details to them.

The elevator doors opened and they were greeted by the same hexagonal room. Strangely, instead of the intricately drawn circle, there was a heptagonal table in the center. It was a deep purplish maroon. At the center lay the strange device.

There were seven chairs around the table. All of them were cushy and comfortable and maroon.

Dr John looked like he'd seen a cat fly.

"This... this was here the whole time?!" he said in a whisper.

"What's with the new arrangement?" said Lily, noticing the absence of the circle.

"Yeah, where did the circle go?" said Sam.

"A circle?" asks Dr John, confused.

"We'll explain," sighs Lily.

"Something is going on," said Sue "I think it has to do with the ritual from before."

"Hmm..." sighs Lily. "I guess there is going to be some sort of conference judging by the layout. We should hide."

They hid behind the same door as before and peeked out every once in a while.

"This is a pretty... um dark place," said Dr John as he looked around the room.

The room looked like a storehouse, filled with alien-looking weapons. The weapons looked nothing like the ones on earth. They were strange... Strange.

They were shaped like normal guns but had curved edges. A deep maroon in colour. There was a small tank filled with a strange yellowish green gel attached to the trigger.

This word kept appearing in their minds.

The circle. The place. The cult.

They heard footsteps from outside as they were taking a look at one of the weapons.

Dr John and Sue rushed to the door to peek through.

Many cult members were scurrying by. They were whispering to each other.

Closely behind them, a strange creature followed.

It had the head of what looked to be an octopus and eight tentacle looking legs. The creature - which they suspected was from Harrison - scuttled behind them with narrow eyes

"What is that thing?" muttered Sam as he got a look of the creature.

"An alien from Harrison," answered Dr John. "I've seen photos but what is it doing here?"

"They are planning something," said Lily, quietly. "Let's stay and find out."

With that, she rushed outside the room and hid behind a box that was lying in front of the door to hide. She listened attentively.

"Lily!" hissed Sue "What are you doing?"

"Getting a better view now, shh!" replied Lily.

XXXI
The New Plan

Meanwhile, all the cult members had settled at the edges. All seven seats were filled. The alien was seated in the centre. The room was quiet. The cult members were silent with anticipation.

The alien said something very quickly. One of the cult members gasped. She then stood up and argued aggressively in the strange language. The alien sighed heavily and glared aggressively.

The cult member was immediately shunned and sat down quickly. The alien then continued after what seemed to be a cough.

It spoke quickly and fluently - much more fluently than the cult members.

The room was silent.

Then the meeting concluded with a formal good-bye.

Lily quickly got behind the door as the entourage of cult members passed by followed by the creature.

"Careful there!" hissed Sue "If you were caught, god knows what would happen!"

"But," argued Lily, in a sly tone, "I saw something important."

"What did you see?" asked Lucy eagerly after her long silence.

"I think we should get out of here," said Dr John "We shouldn't linger or we'll be caught,"

They snuck out when they got the opportunity. As they made their way out, while Lucy went to call the lift, they saw something on the table.

The table had a screen on top of it and it was showing a message which was in the strange language. The message was glitching; changing from one language to the other, waiting for approximately one second and then switching to the next on loop.

At one point, the message was in English. It read:

PLAN EARTH

EXECUTION - TOMORROW 10 AM

RETREAT

Sam, Lily, Sue and Dr John read it.

Lucy had to hiss for them to get into the lift as they just stood there, distracted by the message.

"What was that?" said Sue as the elevator made its way up.

"I don't know," said Lily. "Tomorrow... Something's gonna happen,"

"Stay alert!" said Dr John "I'll be in a meeting when you have your offensive mission later. I will get back from the meeting as soon as I can. Tell me what happens on your mission."

"Yes."

XXXII

What?!

When they got back, Dr John told them to get work. So, as soon as they got back from the block, running, they were rushing to the secret room called 'S 01'.

They quickly went through the security measures and entered.

"Just on time!" Dr Smith greeted them at the entrance. "We are just getting started."

As Dr Smith led them in, they glanced around. The room's layout had changed. There was what looked like a rocket launcher outside a window that hadn't been there the first time they saw the room.

There were a lot of people gathered around the window. Dr Smith ushered them aside to show Team SSTR a control panel. It covered approximately six and a half feet. There were many buttons and screens scattered across the control panel. There were speakers and microphones as well.

Dr Smith walked to it "This is the control panel. We control that thing with it."

"What is that?" asked Sam, in awe at the huge structure.

"That's a government project we were tasked with a few years ago, got it renovated," said Dr Smith "It was called the 'destroyer' before the project was dropped."

"What was it for?" asked Lily "I don't think this is just for friendly fire,"

"Well," said Dr Smith "This was an emergency project... Less about that, now we wait!"

"Wait until what?" asked Sue.

"Until the cult retaliates," said Dr Smith darkly.

"You are going to attack?!" exclaimed Sue "This isn't practical! What happened?!"

"War against a cult or what not they might have on their side isn't practical!" said Lily.

"We'll be able to explain very soon," said Dr Jones from behind them.

Just then a person holding a flag with a strange symbol ran towards the window. When the flag came into view, they saw it was the cult's flag.

"Idiots!"

The sound played on the speakers. Everyone looked out the window. The strange creature from before scuttled to the front beside the person followed by more of the creatures who appeared to be guards. They were carrying the guns from before and stood around the person and creature in the front.

"You refuse to join us in our righteous quest!"

Many other creatures and people came into view. Most of them were holding the flags.

The voice could be heard across the silent room. It was the voice of the old Lauren woman. She was speaking dramatically. As if she were giving a speech. Loud and dramatic with a tone of supremacy. As if she was right.

"Well, we've decided we're over this foolishness! Go ahead and do as you please! But we will be back!"

Nobody said a word. Everyone was confused. What was going on? The cult had been silent for some time.

"This... this is quite unpredictable," Dr Smith muttered under his breath. "Lauren... what consumed you... to become like this,"

He ended his sentence heavily.

"If you wish to attack, do so at your own risk! We have made... alliances..."

There was a slight pause.

Lucy gasped, her face lined with fear.

"While you ponder on this desolate hull of a planet, we shall return to our one true home! And bring back what we so sadly lost, dear humans! Farewell... for now. And wish to see you again."

"Our... home?" muttered Sam, confused under his breath.

"I think... I think this is bigger than it looks," replied Lily, trailing off into a whisper.

Everyone in the room could only stare as the whole group turned their backs to the window and left slowly.

Baffled, everyone in the room just stood there. No one would say a word. They wondered if they had really just heard what they had heard.

A minute or so later, Dr Jones entered the room and hurriedly everyone was told to record the events from before and classify the case as UNSOLVED.

They were then ushered outside the room by Dr Jones and Dr Smith without so much as a word.

A million questions were on everyone's mind. What had just happened? What was the speech about? What did this all mean?

The team rushed back to their dorms quickly. They needed to tell Dr John. This was big!

Once they got back, Sue immediately called Dr John.

"Yes, what is it? I am still in the meeting?" answered Dr John in a confused tone.

"It's urgent! We need to meet you!" exclaimed Sue, for the first time being impatient "It's urgent! Can you come now?"

"Not now, but surely once the meeting has ended. You can tell me now."

"The cult has retreated," said Lily firmly as she snatched the phone from Sue.

"What?"

"Yes!" said Lily urgently "I don't know what this means but it can't be good!"

"I'm coming right away!"

www.ingramcontent.com/pod-product-compliance
Lightning Source LLC
Chambersburg PA
CBHW020930160726
47993CB00005B/2207